JAMES SALTER

DUSK AND OTHER STORIES

PICADOR

First published 1990 by Jonathan Cape

First published by Picador 1994

This edition published 2014 by Picador
an imprint of Pan Macmillan, a division of Macmillan Publishers Limited
Pan Macmillan, 20 New Wharf Road, London N1 9RR
Basingstoke and Oxford
Associated companies throughout the world
www.panmacmillan.com

ISBN 978-1-4472-3945-1

Grateful acknowledgement is made to the *Paris Review*, where 'Am Strande von Tanger',
'The Cinema', 'Via Negativa' and 'The Destruction of the Goetheanum' first appeared;
to *Grand Street*, for the publication of 'Lost Sons', 'Akhnilo' and 'Twenty Minutes';
to *Esquire* for 'Foreign Shores', 'Dusk' and 'American Express';
and to the *Carolina Quarterly*, for the publication of 'Dirt'.

1 3 5 7 9 8 6 4 2

A CIP catalogue record for this book is available from the British Library.

Printed and bound by CPI Group (UK) Ltd, Croydon, CR0 4YY

Visit **www.picador.com** to read more about all our books
and to buy them. You will also find features, author interviews and
news of any author events, and you can sign up for e-newsletters
so that you're always first to hear about our new releases.

CONTENTS

AM STRANDE VON TANGER

Barcelona at dawn. The hotels are dark. All the great avenues are pointing to the sea.

The city is empty. Nico is asleep. She is bound by twisted sheets, by her long hair, by a naked arm which falls from beneath her pillow. She lies still, she does not even breathe.

In a cage outlined beneath a square of silk that is indigo blue and black, her bird sleeps, Kalil. The cage is in an empty fireplace which has been scrubbed clean. There are flowers beside it and a bowl of fruit. Kalil is asleep, his head beneath the softness of a wing.

Malcolm is asleep. His steel-rimmed glasses which he does not need—there is no prescription in them—lie open on the table. He sleeps on his back and his nose rides the dream world like a keel. This nose, his mother's nose or at least a replica of his mother's, is like a theatrical device, a strange decoration that has been pasted on his face. It is the first thing one notices about him. It is the first thing one likes. The nose in a sense is a mark of commitment to life. It is a large nose which cannot be hidden. In addition, his teeth are bad.

At the very top of the four stone spires which Gaudi left unfinished the light has just begun to bring forth gold inscriptions too pale to read. There is no sun. There is only a

1

white silence. Sunday morning, the early morning of Spain. A mist covers all of the hills which surround the city. The stores are closed.

Nico has come out on the terrace after her bath. The towel is wrapped around her, water still glistens on her skin.

"It's cloudy," she says. "It's not a good day for the sea."

Malcolm looks up.

"It may clear," he says.

Morning. Villa-Lobos is playing on the phonograph. The cage is on a stool in the doorway. Malcolm lies in a canvas chair eating an orange. He is in love with the city. He has a deep attachment to it based in part on a story by Paul Morand and also on an incident which occurred in Barcelona years before: one evening in the twilight Antonio Gaudi, mysterious, fragile, even saintlike, the city's great architect, was hit by a streetcar as he walked to church. He was very old, white beard, white hair, dressed in the simplest of clothes. No one recognized him. He lay in the street without even a cab to drive him to the hospital. Finally he was taken to the charity ward. He died the day Malcolm was born.

The apartment is on Avenida General Mitre and her tailor, as Nico calls him, is near Gaudi's cathedral at the other end of town. That's a working-class neighborhood, there's a faint smell of garbage. The site is surrounded by walls. There are quatrefoils printed in the sidewalk. Soaring above everything, the spires. *Sanctus, sanctus,* they cry. They are hollow. The cathedral was never completed, its doors lead both ways into open air. Malcolm has walked, in the calm Barcelona evening, around this empty monument many times. He has stuffed peseta notes, virtually worthless, into the slot marked:

DONATIONS TO CONTINUE THE WORK. It seems on the other side they are simply falling to the ground or, he listens closely, a priest wearing glasses locks them in a wooden box.

Malcolm believes in Malraux and Max Weber: art is the real history of nations. In the details of his person there is evidence of a process not fully complete. It is the making of a man into a true instrument. He is preparing for the arrival of that great artist he one day expects to be, an artist in the truly modern sense which is to say without accomplishments but with the conviction of genius. An artist freed from the demands of craft, an artist of concepts, generosity, his work is the creation of the legend of himself. So long as he is provided with even a single follower he can believe in the sanctity of this design.

He is happy here. He likes the wide, tree-cool avenues, the restaurants, the long evenings. He is deep in the currents of a slow, connubial life.

Nico comes onto the terrace wearing a wheat-colored sweater.

"Would you like a coffee?" she says. "Do you want me to go down for one?"

He thinks for a moment.

"Yes," he says.

"How do you like it?"

"*Solo,*" he says.

"Black."

She likes to do this. The building has a small elevator which rises slowly. When it arrives she steps in and closes the doors carefully behind her. Then, just as slowly, she descends, floor after floor, as if they were decades. She thinks about Malcolm. She thinks about her father and his second wife. She is probably more intelligent than Malcolm, she decides. She is certainly stronger-willed. He, however, is better-looking in a strange way. She has a wide, senseless mouth. He is generous. She knows she is a little dry. She passes the second floor. She looks at herself in the mirror. Of course, one doesn't discover these things right away. It's like a play, it unfolds slowly, scene by scene, the reality of another person changes. Anyway, pure intelligence is not that important. It's an abstract quality. It does not include that cruel, intuitive knowledge of how the new life, a life her father would never understand, should be lived. Malcolm has that.

At ten-thirty, the phone rings. She answers and talks in German, lying on the couch. After it is finished Malcolm calls to her, "Who was that?"

"Do you want to go to the beach?"

"Yes."

"Inge is coming in about an hour," Nico says.

He has heard about her and is curious. Besides, she has a car. The morning, obedient to his desires, has begun to change. There is some early traffic on the avenue beneath. The sun breaks through for a moment, disappears, breaks through again. Far off, beyond his thoughts, the four spires are passing between shadow and glory. In intervals of sunlight the letters on high reveal themselves: *Hosanna.*

Smiling, at noon, Inge arrives. She is in a camel skirt and a blouse with the top buttons undone. She's a bit heavy for the skirt which is very short. Nico introduces them.

"Why didn't you call last night?" Inge asks.

"We were going to call but it got so late. We didn't have dinner till eleven," Nico explains. "I was sure you'd be out."

No. She was waiting at home all night for her boyfriend to call, Inge says. She is fanning herself with a postcard from Madrid. Nico has gone into the bedroom.

"They're such bastards," Inge says. Her voice is raised to carry. "He was supposed to call at eight. He didn't call me until ten. He didn't have time to talk. He was going to call back in a little while. Well, he never called. I finally fell asleep."

Nico puts on a pale grey skirt with many small pleats and a lemon pullover. She looks at the back of herself in the mirror. Her arms are bare. Inge is talking from the front room.

"They don't know how to behave, that's the trouble. They don't have any idea. They go to the Polo Club, that's the only thing they know."

She begins to talk to Malcolm.

"When you go to bed with someone it should be nice afterwards, you should treat each other decently. Not here. They have no respect for a woman."

She has green eyes and white, even teeth. He is thinking of what it would be like to have such a mouth. Her father is supposed to be a surgeon. In Hamburg. Nico says it isn't true.

"They are children here," Inge says. "In Germany, now, you have a little respect. A man doesn't treat you like that, he knows what to do."

"Nico," he calls.

She comes in brushing her hair.

"I am frightening him," Inge explains. "Do you know what I finally did? I called at five in the morning. I said, why didn't you call? I don't know, he said—I could tell he was asleep—what time is it? Five o'clock, I said. Are you angry with me? A little, he said. Good, because I am angry with you. Bang, I hung up."

Nico is closing the doors to the terrace and bringing the cage inside.

"It's warm," Malcolm says, "leave him there. He needs the sunlight."

She looks in at the bird.

"I don't think he's well," she says.

"He's all right."

"The other one died last week," she explains to Inge. "Suddenly. He wasn't even sick."

She closes one door and leaves the other open. The bird sits in the now brilliant sunshine, feathered, serene.

"I don't think they can live alone," she says.

"He's fine," Malcolm assures her. "Look at him."

The sun makes his colors very bright. He sits on the uppermost perch. His eyes have perfect, round lids. He blinks.

The elevator is still at their floor. Inge enters first. Malcolm pulls the narrow doors to. It's like shutting a small cabinet. Faces close together they start down. Malcolm is looking at Inge. She has her own thoughts.

They stop for another coffee at the little bar downstairs. He holds the door open for them to go in. No one is there—a single man reading the newspaper.

"I think I'm going to call him again," Inge says.

"Ask him why he woke you up at five in the morning," Malcolm says.

She laughs.

"Yes," she says. "That's marvelous. That's what I'm going to do."

The telephone is at the far end of the marble counter, but Nico is talking to him and he cannot hear.

"Aren't you interested?" he asks.

"No," she says.

Inge's car is a blue Volkswagen, the blue of certain airmail envelopes. One fender is dented in.

"You haven't seen my car," she says. "What do you think? Did I get a good bargain? I don't know anything about cars. This is my first. I bought it from someone I know, a painter, but it was in an accident. The motor is scorched.

"I know how to drive," she says. "It's better if someone sits next to me, though. Can you drive?"

"Of course," he says.

He gets behind the wheel and starts the engine. Nico is sitting in the back.

"How does it feel to you?" Inge says.

"I'll tell you in a minute."

Although it's only a year old, the car has a certain shabbiness. The material on the ceiling is faded. Even the steering wheel seems abused. After they have driven a few blocks, Malcolm says, "It seems all right."

"Yes?"

"The brakes are a little weak."

"They are?"

"I think they need new linings."

"I just had it greased," she says.

Malcolm looks at her. She is quite serious.

"Turn left here," she says.

She directs him through the city. There is a little traffic now but he seldom stops. Many intersections in Barcelona are widened out in the shape of an octagon. There are only a few red lights. They drive through vast neighborhoods of old apartments, past factories, the first vacant fields at the edge of town. Inge turns in her seat to look back to Nico.

"I'm sick of this place," she says. "I want to go to Rome."

They are passing the airport. The road to the sea is crowded. All the scattered traffic of the city has funneled onto it, buses, trucks, innumerable small cars.

"They don't even know how to drive," Inge says. "What are they doing? Can't you pass?

"Oh, come on," she says. She reaches across him to blow the horn.

"No use doing that," Malcolm says.

Inge blows it again.

"They can't move."

"Oh, they make me furious," she cries.

Two children in the car ahead have turned around. Their faces are pale and reflective in the small rear window.

"Have you been to Sitges?" Inge says.

"Cadaques."

"Ah," she says. "Yes. Beautiful. There you have to know someone with a villa."

The sun is white. The land lies beneath it the color of straw. The road runs parallel to the coast past cheap bathing beaches, campgrounds, houses, hotels. Between the road and the sea is the railroad with small tunnels built beneath it for bathers to reach the water. After a while this begins to disappear. They drive along almost deserted stretches.

"In Sitges," Inge says, "are all the blonde girls of Europe. Sweden, Germany, Holland. You'll see."

Malcolm watches the road.

"The brown eyes of the Spaniards are irresistible to them," she says.

She reaches across him to blow the horn.

"Look at them! Look at them crawling along!

"They come here full of hopes," Inge says. "They save their money, they buy little bathing suits you could put in a spoon, and what happens? They get loved for one night, perhaps, that's all. The Spanish don't know how to treat women."

Nico is silent in the back. On her face is the calm expression which means she is bored.

"They know nothing," Inge says.

Sitges is a little town with damp hotels, the green shutters, the dying grass of a beach resort. There are cars parked everywhere. The streets are lined with them. Finally they find a place two blocks from the sea.

"Be sure it's locked," Inge says.

"Nobody's going to steal it," Malcolm tells her.

"Now you don't think it's so nice," she says.

They walk along the pavement, the surface of which seems to have buckled in the heat. All around are the flat, undecorated facades of houses built too close together. Despite the cars, the town is strangely vacant. It's two o'clock. Everyone is at lunch.

Malcolm has a pair of shorts made from rough cotton, the blue glazed cotton of the Tuaregs. They have a little belt, slim as a finger, which goes only halfway around. He feels powerful as he puts them on. He has a runner's body, a body without flaws, the body of a martyr in a Flemish painting. One can see vessels laid like cord beneath the surface of his limbs. The cabins have a concrete back wall and hemp underfoot. His clothes hang shapeless from a peg. He steps into the corridor. The women are still undressing, he does not know behind which door. There is a small mirror hung from a nail. He smooths his hair and waits. Outside is the sun.

The sea begins with a sloping course of pebbles sharp as nails. Malcolm goes in first. Nico follows without a word. The water is cool. He feels it climb his legs, touch the edge of his suit and then with a swell—he tries to leap high enough—embrace him. He dives. He comes up smiling. The taste of salt is on his lips. Nico has dived, too. She emerges close by, softly, and draws her wetted hair behind her with one hand. She stands with her eyes half-closed, not knowing exactly where she is. He slips an arm around her waist. She smiles. She possesses a certain, sure instinct of when she is most beautiful. For a moment they are in serene dependence. He lifts her in his arms and carries her, helped by the sea, toward the deep. Her head rests on his shoulder. Inge lies on the beach in her bikini reading *Stern*.

"What's wrong with Inge?" he says.

"Everything."

"No, doesn't she want to come in?"

"She's having her period," Nico says.

They lie down beside her on separate towels. She is,

Malcolm notices, very brown. Nico can never get that way no matter how long she stays outside. It is almost a kind of stubbornness as if he, himself, were offering her the sun and she would not accept.

She got this tan in a single day, Inge tells them. A single day! It seems unbelievable. She looks at her arms and legs as if confirming it. Yes, it's true. Naked on the rocks at Cadaques. She looks down at her stomach and in doing so induces it to reveal several plump, girlish rolls.

"You're getting fat," Nico says.

Inge laughs. "They are my savings," she says.

They seem like that, like belts, like part of some costume she is wearing. When she lies back, they are gone. Her limbs are clean. Her stomach, like the rest of her, is covered with a faint, golden down. Two Spanish youths are strolling past along the sea.

She is talking to the sky. If she goes to America, she recites, is it worthwhile to bring her car? After all, she got it at a very good price, she could probably sell it if she didn't want to keep it and make some money.

"America is full of Volkswagens," Malcolm says.

"Yes?"

"It's filled with German cars, everyone has one."

"They must like them," she decides. "The Mercedes is a good car."

"Greatly admired," Malcolm says.

"That's the car I would like. I would like a couple of them. When I have money, that will be my hobby," she says. "I'd like to live in Tangier."

"Quite a beach there."

"Yes? I will be black as an Arab."

"Better wear your suit," Malcolm says.

Inge smiles.

Nico seems asleep. They lie there silent, their feet pointed to the sun. The strength of it has gone. There are only passing moments of warmth when the wind dies all the way and the sun is flat upon them, weak but flooding. An hour of melancholy is approaching, the hour when everything is ended.

At six o'clock Nico sits up. She is cold.

"Come," Inge says, "we'll go for a walk up the beach."

She insists on it. The sun has not set. She becomes very playful.

"Come," she says, "it's the good section, all the big villas are there. We'll walk along and make the old men happy."

"I don't want to make anyone happy," Nico says, hugging her arms.

"It isn't so easy," Inge assures her.

Nico goes along sullenly. She is holding her elbows. The wind is from the shore. There are little waves now which seem to break in silence. The sound they make is soft, as if forgotten. Nico is wearing a grey tank suit with an open back, and while Inge plays before the houses of the rich, she looks at the sand.

Inge goes into the sea. Come, she says, it's warm. She is laughing and happy, her gaiety is stronger than the hour, stronger than the cold. Malcolm walks slowly in behind her. The water *is* warm. It seems purer as well. And it is empty, as far in each direction as one can see. They are bathing in it alone. The waves swell and lift them gently. The water runs over them, laving the soul.

At the entrance to the cabins the young Spanish boys stand around waiting for a glimpse if the shower door is opened too soon. They wear blue woolen trunks. Also black. Their feet appear to have very long toes. There is only one shower and in it a single, whitened tap. The water is cold. Inge goes first. Her suit appears, one small piece and then the other, draped over the top of the door. Malcolm waits. He can hear the soft slap and passage of her hands, the sudden shattering of the water on concrete when she moves aside. The boys at the door exalt him. He glances out. They are talking in low voices. They reach out to tease each other, to make an appearance of play.

The streets of Sitges have changed. An hour has struck which announces evening, and everywhere there are strolling crowds. It's difficult to stay together. Malcolm has an arm around each of them. They drift to his touch like horses. Inge smiles. People will think the three of them do it together, she says.

They stop at a café. It isn't a good one, Inge complains.

"It's the best," Nico says simply. It is one of her qualities that she can tell at a glance, wherever she goes, which is the right place, the right restaurant, hotel.

"No," Inge insists.

Nico seems not to care. They wander on separated now, and Malcolm whispers, "What is she looking for?"

"Don't you know?" Nico says.

"You see these boys?" Inge says. They are seated in another place, a bar. All around them, tanned limbs, hair faded from the long, baking afternoons, young men sit with the sweet stare of indolence.

"They have no money," she says. "None of them could take you to dinner. Not one of them. They have nothing. This is Spain," she says.

Nico chooses the place for dinner. She has become a lesser person during the day. The presence of this friend, this girl she casually shared a life with during the days they both were struggling to find themselves in the city, before she knew anybody or even the names of streets, when she was so sick that they wrote out a cable to her father together—they had no telephone—this sudden revelation of Inge seems to have deprived the past of decency. All at once she is pierced by a certainty that Malcolm feels contempt for her. Her confidence, without which she is nothing, has gone. The tablecloth seems white and dazzling. It seems to be illuminating the three of them with remorseless light. The knives and forks are laid out as if for surgery. The plates lie cold. She is not hungry but she doesn't dare refuse to eat. Inge is talking about her boyfriend.

"He is terrible," she says, "he is heartless. But I understand him. I know what he wants. Anyway, a woman can't hope to be everything to a man. It isn't natural. A man needs a number of women."

"You're crazy," Nico says flatly.

"It's true."

The statement is all that was needed to demoralize her. Malcolm is inspecting the strap of his watch. It seems to Nico he is permitting all this. He is stupid, she thinks. This girl is from a low background and he finds that interesting. She thinks because they go to bed with her they will marry her. Of course not. Never. Nothing, Nico thinks, could be farther from the truth, though even as she thinks she knows she may be wrong.

They go to Chez Swann for a coffee. Nico sits apart. She is tired, she says. She curls up on one of the couches and goes to sleep. She is exhausted. The evening has become quite cool.

A voice awakens her, music, a marvelous voice amid occasional phrases of the guitar. Nico hears it in her sleep and sits up. Malcolm and Inge are talking. The song is like something long-awaited, something she has been searching for. She reaches over and touches his arm.

"Listen," she says.

"What?"

"Listen," she says, "it's Maria Pradera."

"Maria Pradera?"

"The words are beautiful," Nico says.

Simple phrases. She repeats them, as if they were litany. Mysterious repetitions: dark-haired mother . . . dark-haired child. The eloquence of the poor, worn smooth and pure as a stone.

Malcolm listens patiently but he hears nothing. She can see it: he has changed, he has been poisoned while she slept with stories of a hideous Spain fed bit by bit until now they are drifting through his veins, a Spain devised by a woman who knows she can never be more than part of what a man needs. Inge is calm. She believes in herself. She believes in her right to exist, to command.

The road is dark. They have opened the roof to the night,

a night so dense with stars that they seem to be pouring into the car. Nico, in the back, feels frightened. Inge is talking. She reaches over to blow the horn at cars which are going too slow. Malcolm laughs at it. There are private rooms in Barcelona where, with her lover, Inge spent winter afternoons before a warm, crackling fire. There are houses where they made love on blankets of fur. Of course, he was nice then. She had visions of the Polo Club, of dinner parties in the best houses.

The streets of the city are almost deserted. It is nearly midnight, Sunday midnight. The day in the sun has wearied them, the sea has drained them of strength. They drive to General Mitre and say good night through the windows of the car. The elevator rises very slowly. They are hung with silence. They look at the floor like gamblers who have lost.

The apartment is dark. Nico turns on a light and then vanishes. Malcolm washes his hands. He dries them. The rooms seem very still. He begins to walk through them slowly and finds her, as if she had fallen, on her knees in the doorway to the terrace.

Malcolm looks at the cage. Kalil has fallen to the floor.

"Give him a little brandy on the corner of a handkerchief," he says.

She has opened the cage door.

"He's dead," she says.

"Let me see."

He is stiff. The small feet are curled and dry as twigs. He seems lighter somehow. The breath has left his feathers. A heart no bigger than an orange seed has ceased to beat. The cage sits empty in the cold doorway. There seems nothing to say. Malcolm closes the door.

Later, in bed, he listens to her sobs. He tries to comfort her but he cannot. Her back is turned to him. She will not answer.

She has small breasts and large nipples. Also, as she herself says, a rather large behind. Her father has three secretaries. Hamburg is close to the sea.

TWENTY MINUTES

This happened near Carbondale to a woman named Jane Vare. I met her once at a party. She was sitting on a couch with her arms stretched out on either side and a drink in one hand. We talked about dogs.

She had an old greyhound. She'd bought him to save his life, she said. At the tracks they put them down rather than feed them when they stopped winning, sometimes three or four together, threw them in the back of a truck and drove to the dump. This dog was named Phil. He was stiff and nearly blind, but she admired his dignity. He sometimes lifted his leg against the wall, almost as high as the door handle, but he had a fine face.

Tack on the kitchen table, mud on the wide-board floor. In she strode like a young groom in a worn jacket and boots. She had what they called a good seat and ribbons layered like feathers on the wall. Her father had lived in Ireland where they rode into the dining room on Sunday morning and the host died fallen on the bed in full attire. Her own life had become like that. Money and dents in the side of her nearly new Swedish car. Her husband had been gone for a year.

Around Carbondale the river drops down and widens.

There's a spidery trestle bridge, many times repainted, and they used to mine coal.

It was late in the afternoon and a shower had passed. The light was silvery and strange. Cars emerging from the rain drove with their headlights on and the windshield wipers going. The yellow road machinery parked along the shoulder seemed unnaturally bright.

It was the hour after work when irrigation water glistens high in the air, the hills have begun to darken and the meadows are like ponds.

She was riding alone up along the ridge. She was on a horse named Fiume, big, well formed, but not very smart. He didn't hear things and sometimes stumbled when he walked. They had gone as far as the reservoir and then come back, riding to the west where the sun was going down. He could run, this horse. His hooves were pounding. The back of her shirt was filled with wind, the saddle was creaking, his huge neck was dark with sweat. They came along the ditch and toward a gate—they jumped it all the time.

At the last moment something happened. It took just an instant. He may have crossed his legs or hit a hole but he suddenly gave way. She went over his head and as if in slow motion he came after. He was upside down—she lay there watching him float toward her. He landed on her open lap.

It was as if she'd been hit by a car. She was stunned but felt unhurt. For a minute she imagined she might stand up and brush herself off.

The horse had gotten up. His legs were dirty and there

was dirt on his back. In the silence she could hear the clink of the bridle and even the water flowing in the ditch. All around her were meadows and stillness. She felt sick to her stomach. It was all broken down there—she knew it although she could feel nothing. She knew she had some time. Twenty minutes, they always said.

The horse was pulling at some grass. She rose to her elbows and was immediately dizzy. "God damn you!" she called. She was nearly crying. "Git! Go home!" Someone might see the empty saddle. She closed her eyes and tried to think. Somehow she could not believe it—nothing that had happened was true.

It was that way the morning they came and told her Privet had been hurt. The foreman was waiting in the pasture. "Her leg's broken," he said.

"How did it happen?"

He didn't know. "It looks like she got kicked," he guessed.

The horse was lying under a tree. She knelt and stroked its boardlike nose. The large eyes seemed to be looking elsewhere. The vet would be driving up from Catherine Store trailing a plume of dust, but it turned out to be a long time before he came. He parked a little way off and walked over. Afterward he said what she had known he would say, they were going to have to put her down.

She lay remembering that. The day had ended. Lights were appearing in parts of distant houses. The six o'clock news was on. Far below she could see the hayfield of Piñones and much closer, a hundred yards off, a truck. It belonged to someone trying to build a house down there. It was up on blocks, it didn't run. There were other houses within a mile or so. On the other side of the ridge the metal roof, hidden in trees, of old man Vaughn who had once owned all of this and now could hardly walk. Further west the beautiful tan adobe Bill Millinger built before he went broke or whatever it was. He had wonderful taste. The house had the peeled log ceilings of the Southwest, Navajo rugs, and fireplaces in every room. Wide views of the mountains through windows of tinted glass. Anyone who knew enough to build a house like that knew everything.

She had given the famous dinner for him, unforgettable night. The clouds had been blowing off the top of Sopris all day, then came the snow. They talked in front of the fire. There were wine bottles crowded on the mantle and everyone in good clothes. Outside the snow poured down. She was wearing silk pants and her hair was loose. In the end she stood with him near the doorway to her kitchen. She was filled with warmth and a little drunk, was he?

He was watching her finger on the edge of his jacket lapel. Her heart thudded. "You're not going to make me spend the night alone?" she asked.

He had blond hair and small ears close to his head. "Oh . . ." he began.

"What?"

"Don't you know? I'm the other way."

Which way, she insisted. It was such a waste. The roads were almost closed, the house lost in snow. She began to plead—she couldn't help it—and then became angry. The silk pants, the furniture, she hated it all.

In the morning his car was outside. She found him in the kitchen making breakfast. He'd slept on the couch, combed his longish hair with his fingers. On his cheeks was a blond stubble. "Sleep well, darling?" he asked.

Sometimes it was the other way around—in Saratoga in the bar where the idol was the tall Englishman who had made so much money at the sales. Did she live there? he asked. When you were close his eyes looked watery but in that English voice which was so pure, "It's marvelous to come to a place and see someone like you," he said.

She hadn't really decided whether to stay or leave and she had a drink with him. He smoked a cigarette.

"You haven't heard about those?" she said.

"No, what about them?"

"They'll give thee cancer."

"Thee?"

"It's what the Quakers say."

"Are you really a Quaker?"

"Oh, back a ways."

He had her by the elbow. "Do you know what I'd like? I'd like to fuck thee," he said.

She bent her arm to remove it.

"I mean it," he said. "Tonight."

"Some other time," she told him.

"I don't have another time. My wife's coming tomorrow, I only have tonight."

"That's too bad. I have every night."

She hadn't forgotten him, though she'd forgotten his name. His shirt had elegant blue stripes. "Oh, damn you," she suddenly cried. It was the horse. He hadn't gone. He was over by the fence. She began to call him, "Here, boy. Come here," she begged. He wouldn't move.

She didn't know what to do. Five minutes had passed, perhaps longer. Oh, God, she said, oh, Lord, oh God our Father. She could see the long stretch of road that came up from the highway, the unpaved surface very pale. Someone would come up that road and not turn off. The disastrous road. She had been driving it that day with her husband. There was something he had been meaning to tell her, Henry said, his head tilted back at a funny angle. He was making a change in his life. Her heart took a skip. He was breaking off with Mara, he said.

There was a silence.

Finally she said, "With who?"

He realized his mistake. "The girl who . . . in the architect's office. She's the draftsman."

"What do you mean, breaking it off?" It was hard for her to speak. She was looking at him as one would look at a fugitive.

"You knew about that, didn't you? I was sure you knew. Anyway it's over. I wanted to tell you. I wanted to put it all behind us."

"Stop the car," she said. "Don't say any more, stop here."

He drove alongside her trying to explain but she was picking up the biggest stones she could find and throwing them at the car. Then she cut unsteadily across the fields, the sage bushes scratching her legs.

When she heard him drive up after midnight she jumped from bed and shouted from the window, "No, no! Go away!"

"What I never understood is why no one told me," she used to say. "They were supposed to be my friends."

Some failed, some divorced, some got shot in trailers like

Doug Portis who had the excavation business and was seeing the policeman's wife. Some like her husband moved to Santa Barbara and became the extra man at dinner parties.

It was growing dark. Help me, someone, help me, she kept repeating. Someone would come, they had to. She tried not to be afraid. She thought of her father who could explain life in one sentence, "They knock you down and you get up. That's what it's all about." He recognized only one virtue. He would hear what had happened, that she merely lay there. She had to try to get home, even if she went only a little way, even a few yards.

Pushing with her palms she managed to drag herself, calling the horse as she did. Perhaps she could grab a stirrup if he came. She tried to find him. In the last of the light she saw the fading cottonwoods but the rest had disappeared. The fence posts were gone. The meadows had drifted away.

She tried to play a game, she wasn't lying near the ditch, she was in another place, in all the places, on Eleventh Street in that first apartment above the big skylight of the restaurant, the morning in Sausalito with the maid knocking on the door and Henry trying to call in Spanish, not now, not now! And postcards on the marble of the dresser and things they'd bought. Outside the hotel in Haiti the cabdrivers were leaning on their cars and calling out in soft voices, Hey, *blanc*, you like to go to a nice beach? Ibo beach? They wanted thirty dollars for the day, they said, which meant the price was probably about five. Go ahead, give it to him, she said. She could be there so easily, or in her own bed reading on a stormy day with the rain gusting against the window and the dogs near her feet. On the desk were photographs: horses, and her jumping, and one of her father at lunch outside when he was thirty, at Burning Tree. She had called him one day—she was getting married, she said. Married, he said, to whom? A man named Henry Vare, she said, who is wearing a beautiful suit, she wanted to add, and has wonderful wide hands. Tomorrow, she said.

"Tomorrow?" He sounded farther away. "Are you sure you're doing the right thing?"

"Absolutely."

"God bless you," he said.

That summer was the one they came here—it was where Henry had been living—and bought the place past the Macraes'. All year they fixed up the house and Henry started his landscaping business. They had their own world. Up through the fields in nothing but shorts, the earth warm under their feet, skin flecked with dirt from swimming in the ditch where the water was chilly and deep, like two sun-bleached children but far better, the screen door slamming, things on the kitchen table, catalogues, knives, new everything. Autumn with its brilliant blue skies and the first storms coming up from the west.

It was dark now, everywhere except up by the ridge. There were all the things she had meant to do, to go East again, to visit certain friends, to live a year by the sea. She could not believe it was over, that she was going to be left here on the ground.

Suddenly she started to call for help, wildly, the cords standing out in her neck. In the darkness the horse raised his head. She kept shouting. She already knew it was a thing she would pay for, she was loosing the demonic. At last she stopped. She could hear the pounding of her heart and beyond that something else. Oh, God, she began to beg. Lying there she heard the first solemn drumbeats, terrible and slow.

Whatever it was, however bad, I'm going to do it as my father would, she thought. Hurriedly she tried to imagine him and as she was doing it a length of something went through her, something iron. In one unbelievable instant she realized the power of it, where it would take her, what it meant.

Her face was wet and she was shivering. Now it was here. Now you must do it, she realized. She knew there was a God, she hoped it. She shut her eyes. When she opened them it had begun, so utterly unforeseen and with such speed. She saw something dark moving along the fence line. It was her pony, the one her father had given her long ago, her black pony going home, across the broad fields, across the grassland. Wait, wait for me!

She began to scream.

Lights were jerking up and down along the ditch. It was a pickup coming over the uneven ground, the man who was sometimes building the lone house and a high school girl named Fern who worked at the golf course. They had the windows up and, turning, their lights swept close to the horse but they didn't see him. They saw him later, coming back in silence, the big handsome face in the darkness looking at them dumbly.

"He's saddled," Fern said in surprise.

He was standing calmly. That was how they found her. They put her in the back—she was limp, there was dirt in her ears—and drove into Glenwood at eighty miles an hour, not even stopping to call ahead.

That wasn't the right thing, as someone said later. It would have been better if they had gone the other way, about three miles up the road to Bob Lamb's. He was the vet but he might have done something. Whatever you said, he was the best doctor around.

They would have pulled in with the headlights blooming on the white farmhouse as happened so many nights. Everyone knew Bob Lamb. There were a hundred dogs, his own among them, buried in back of the barn.

AMERICAN EXPRESS

It's hard now to think of all the places and nights, Nicola's like a railway car, deep and gleaming, the crowd at the *Un, Deux, Trois*, Billy's. Unknown brilliant faces jammed at the bar. The dark, dramatic eye that blazes for a moment and disappears.

In those days they were living in apartments with funny furniture and on Sundays sleeping until noon. They were in the last rank of the armies of law. Clever junior partners were above them, partners, associates, men in fine suits who had lunch at the Four Seasons. Frank's father went there three or four times a week, or else to the Century Club or the Union where there were men even older than he. Half of the members can't urinate, he used to say, and the other half can't stop.

Alan, on the other hand, was from Cleveland where his father was well known, if not detested. No defendant was too guilty, no case too clear-cut. Once in another part of the state he was defending a murderer, a black man. He knew what the jury was thinking, he knew what he looked like to them. He stood up slowly. It could be they had heard certain things, he began. They may have heard, for instance, that he was a big-time lawyer from the city. They may have heard that he wore three-hundred-dollar suits, that he drove a Cadillac and smoked expensive cigars. He was walking along as if looking for something on the floor. They may have heard that he was Jewish.

He stopped and looked up. Well, he was from the city, he said. He wore three-hundred-dollar suits, he drove a Cadillac, smoked big cigars, and he was Jewish. "Now that we have that settled, let's talk about this case."

Lawyers and sons of lawyers. Days of youth. In the morning in stale darkness the subways shrieked.

"Have you noticed the new girl at the reception desk?"

"What about her?" Frank asked.

They were surrounded by noise like the launch of a rocket. "She's hot," Alan confided.

"How do you know?"

"I know."

"What do you mean, you know?"

"Intuition."

"Intuition?" Frank said.

"What's wrong?"

"That doesn't count."

Which was what made them inseparable, the hours of work, the lyric, the dreams. As it happened, they never knew the girl at the reception desk with her nearsightedness and wild, full hair. They knew various others, they knew Julie, they knew Catherine, they knew Ames. The best, for nearly two years, was Brenda who had somehow managed to graduate from Marymount and had a walk-through apartment on West Fourth. In a smooth, thin, silver frame was the photograph of her father with his two daughters at the Plaza, Brenda, thirteen, with an odd little smile.

"I wish I'd known you then," Frank told her.

Brenda said, "I bet you do."

It was her voice he liked, the city voice, scornful and warm. They were two of a kind, she liked to say, and in a way it was true. They drank in her favorite places where the owner played the piano and everyone seemed to know her. Still, she counted on him. The city has its incomparable moments— rolling along the wall of the apartment, kissing, bumping like stones. Five in the afternoon, the vanishing light. "No," she was commanding. "No, no, no."

He was kissing her throat. "What are you going to do with that beautiful struma of yours?"

"You won't take me to dinner," she said.

"Sure I will."

"Beautiful what?"

She was like a huge dog, leaping from his arms.

"Come here," he coaxed.

She went into the bathroom and began combing her hair. "Which restaurant are we going to?" she called.

She would give herself but it was mostly unpredictable. She would do anything her mother hadn't done and would live as her mother lived, in the same kind of apartment, in the same soft chairs. Christmas and the envelopes for the doormen, the snow sweeping past the awning, her children coming home from school. She adored her father. She went on a trip to Hawaii with him and sent back postcards, two or three scorching lines in a large, scrawled hand.

It was summer.

"Anybody here?" Frank called.

He rapped on the door which was ajar. He was carrying his jacket, it was hot.

"All right," he said in a loud voice, "come out with your hands over your head. Alan, cover the back."

The party, it seemed, was over. He pushed the door open. There was one lamp on, the room was dark.

"Hey, Bren, are we too late?" he called. She appeared mysteriously in the doorway, barelegged but in heels. "We'd have come earlier but we were working. We couldn't get out of the office. Where is everybody? Where's all the food? Hey, Alan, we're late. There's no food, nothing."

She was leaning against the doorway.

"We tried to get down here," Alan said. "We couldn't get a cab."

Frank had fallen onto the couch. "Bren, don't be mad," he said. "We were working, that's the truth. I should have called. Can you put some music on or something? Is there anything to drink?"

"There's about that much vodka," she finally said.

"Any ice?"

"About two cubes." She pushed off the wall without much enthusiasm. He watched her walk into the kitchen and heard the refrigerator door open.

"So, what do you think, Alan?" he said. "What are you going to do?"

"Me?"

"Where's Louise?" Frank called.

"Asleep," Brenda said.

"Did she really go home?"

"She goes to work in the morning."

"So does Alan."

Brenda came out of the kitchen with the drinks.

"I'm sorry we're late," he said. He was looking in the glass. "Was it a good party?" He stirred the contents with one finger. "This is the ice?"

"Jane Harrah got fired," Brenda said.

"That's too bad. Who is she?"

"She does big campaigns. Ross wants me to take her place."

"Great."

"I'm not sure if I want to," she said lazily.

"Why not?"

"She was sleeping with him."

"And she got fired?"

"Doesn't say much for him, does it?"

"It doesn't say much for her."

"That's just like a man. God."

"What does she look like? Does she look like Louise?"

The smile of the thirteen-year-old came across Brenda's face. "No one looks like Louise," she said. Her voice squeezed the name whose legs Alan dreamed of. "Jane has these thin lips."

"Is that all?"

"Thin-lipped women are always cold."

"Let me see yours," he said.

"Burn up."

"Yours aren't thin. Alan, these aren't thin, are they? Hey, Brenda, don't cover them up."

"Where were you? You weren't really working."

He'd pulled down her hand. "Come on, let them be

natural," he said. "They're not thin, they're nice. I just never noticed them before." He leaned back. "Alan, how're you doing? You getting sleepy?"

"I was thinking. How much the city has changed," Alan said.

"In five years?"

"I've been here almost six years."

"Sure, it's changing. They're coming down, we're going up."

Alan was thinking of the vanished Louise who had left him only a jolting ride home through the endless streets. "I know."

That year they sat in the steam room on limp towels, breathing the eucalyptus and talking about Hardmann Roe. They walked to the showers like champions. Their flesh still had firmness. Their haunches were solid and young.

Hardmann Roe was a small drug company in Connecticut that had strayed slightly outside of its field and found itself suing a large manufacturer for infringement of an obscure patent. The case was highly technical with little chance of success. The opposing lawyers had thrown up a barricade of motions and delays and the case had made its way downwards, to Frik and Frak whose offices were near the copying machines, who had time for such things, and who pondered it amid the hiss of steam. No one else wanted it and this also made it appealing.

So they worked. They were students again, sitting around in polo shirts with their feet on the desk, throwing off hopeless ideas, crumpling wads of paper, staying late in the library and having the words blur in books.

They stayed on through vacations and weekends, sometimes sleeping in the office and making coffee long before anyone came to work. After a late dinner they were still talking about it, its complexities, where elements somehow fit in, the sequence of letters, articles in journals, meetings, the limits of meaning. Brenda met a handsome Dutchman who worked for a bank. Alan met Hopie. Still there was this infinite forest, the trunks and vines blocking out the light, the roots of distant things joined. With every month that passed they were deeper into it, less certain of where they had been or if it could end. They had become like the old partners whose existence had been slowly sealed off, fewer calls, fewer consultations, lives that had become lunch. It was known they were swallowed up by the case with knowledge of little else. The opposite was true—no one else understood its details. Three years had passed. The length of time alone made it important. The reputation of the firm, at least in irony, was riding on them.

Two months before the case was to come to trial they quit Weyland, Braun. Frank sat down at the polished table for Sunday lunch. His father was one of the best men in the city. There is a kind of lawyer you trust and who becomes your friend. "What happened?" he wanted to know.

"We're starting our own firm," Frank said.

"What about the case you've been working on? You can't leave them with a litigation you've spent years preparing."

"We're not. We're taking it with us," Frank said.

There was a moment of dreadful silence.

"Taking it with you? You can't. You went to one of the best schools, Frank. They'll sue you. You'll ruin yourself."

"We thought of that."

"Listen to me," his father said.

Everyone said that, his mother, his Uncle Cook, friends. It was worse than ruin, it was dishonor. His father said that.

Hardmann Roe never went to trial, as it turned out. Six weeks later there was a settlement. It was for thirty-eight million, a third of it their fee.

His father had been wrong, which was something you could not hope for. They weren't sued either. That was settled, too. In place of ruin there were new offices overlooking Bryant Park which from above seemed like a garden behind a dark château, young clients, opera tickets, dinners in apartments with divorced hostesses, surrendered apartments with books and big, tiled kitchens.

The city was divided, as he had said, into those going up and those coming down, those in crowded restaurants and those on the street, those who waited and those who did not, those with three locks on the door and those rising in an elevator from a lobby with silver mirrors and walnut paneling.

And those like Mrs. Christie who was in the intermediate state though looking assured. She wanted to renegotiate the settlement with her ex-husband. Frank had leafed through the papers. "What do you think?" she asked candidly.

"I think it would be easier for you to get married again."

She was in her fur coat, the dark lining displayed. She gave a little puff of disbelief. "It's not that easy," she said.

He didn't know what it was like, she told him. Not long ago she'd been introduced to someone by a couple she knew very well. "We'll go to dinner," they said, "you'll love him, you're perfect for him, he likes to talk about books."

They arrived at the apartment and the two women immediately went into the kitchen and began cooking. What did she think of him? She'd only had a glimpse, she said, but she liked him very much, his beautiful bald head, his dressing gown. She had begun to plan what she would do with the apartment which had too much blue in it. The man—Warren was his name—was silent all evening. He'd lost his job, her friend explained in the kitchen. Money was no problem, but he was depressed. "He's had a shock," she said. "He likes you." And in fact he'd asked if he could see her again.

"Why don't you come for tea, tomorrow?" he said.

"I could do that," she said. "Of course. I'll be in the neighborhood," she added.

The next day she arrived at four with a bag filled with books, at least a hundred dollars' worth which she'd bought as a present. He was in pajamas. There was no tea. He hardly seemed to know who she was or why she was there. She said she remembered she had to meet someone and left the books. Going down in the elevator she felt suddenly sick to her stomach.

"Well," said Frank, "there might be a chance of getting the settlement overturned, Mrs. Christie, but it would mean a lot of expense."

"I see." Her voice was smaller. "Couldn't you do it as one of those things where you got a percentage?"

"Not on this kind of case," he said.

It was dusk. He offered her a drink. She worked her lips,

in contemplation, one against the other. "Well, then, what can I do?"

Her life had been made up of disappointments, she told him, looking into her glass, most of them the result of foolishly falling in love. Going out with an older man just because he was wearing a white suit in Nashville which was where she was from. Agreeing to marry George Christie while they were sailing off the coast of Maine. "I don't know where to get the money," she said, "or how."

She glanced up. She found him looking at her, without haste. The lights were coming on in buildings surrounding the park, in the streets, on homeward bound cars. They talked as evening fell. They went out to dinner.

At Christmas that year Alan and his wife broke up. "You're kidding," Frank said. He'd moved into a new place with thick towels and fine carpets. In the foyer was a Biedermeier desk, black, tan, and gold. Across the street was a private school.

Alan was staring out the window which was as cold as the side of a ship. "I don't know what to do," he said in despair. "I don't want to get divorced. I don't want to lose my daughter." Her name was Camille. She was two.

"I know how you feel," Frank said.

"If you had a kid, you'd know."

"Have you seen this?" Frank asked. He held up the alumni magazine. It was the fifteenth anniversary of their graduation. "Know any of these guys?"

Five members of the class had been cited for achievement. Alan recognized two or three of them. "Cummings," he said, "he was a zero—elected to Congress. Oh, God, I don't know what to do."

"Just don't let her take the apartment," Frank said.

Of course, it wasn't that easy. It was easy when it was someone else. Nan Christie had decided to get married. She brought it up one evening.

"I just don't think so," he finally said.

"You love me, don't you?"

"This isn't a good time to ask."

They lay silently. She was staring at something across the room. She was making him feel uncomfortable. "It wouldn't work. It's the attraction of opposites," he said.

"We're not opposites."

"I don't mean just you and me. Women fall in love when they get to know you. Men are just the opposite. When they finally know you they're ready to leave."

She got up without saying anything and began gathering her clothes. He watched her dress in silence. There was nothing interesting about it. The funny thing was that he had meant to go on with her.

"I'll get you a cab," he said.

"I used to think that you were intelligent," she said, half to herself. Exhausted, he was searching for a number. "I don't want a cab. I'm going to walk."

"Across the park?"

"Yes." She had an instant glimpse of herself in the next day's paper. She paused at the door for a moment. "Goodbye," she said coolly.

She wrote him a letter which he read several times. *Of all the loves I have known, none has touched me so. Of all the men, no one has given me more.* He showed it to Alan who did not comment.

"Let's go out and have a drink," Frank said.

They walked up Lexington. Frank looked carefree, the scarf around his neck, the open topcoat, the thinning hair. "Well, you know . . ." he managed to say.

They went into a place called Jack's. Light was gleaming from the dark wood and the lines of glasses on narrow shelves. The young bartender stood with his hands on the edge of the bar. "How are you this evening?" he said with a smile. "Nice to see you again."

"Do you know me?" Frank asked.

"You look familiar," the bartender smiled.

"Do I? What's the name of this place, anyway? Remind me not to come in here again."

There were several other people at the bar. The nearest of them carefully looked away. After a while the manager came over. He had emerged from the brown-curtained back. "Anything wrong, sir?" he asked politely.

Frank looked at him. "No," he said, "everything's fine."

"We've had a big day," Alan explained. "We're just unwinding."

"We have a dining room upstairs," the manager said. Behind him was an iron staircase winding past framed drawings of dogs—borzois they looked like. "We serve from six to eleven every night."

"I bet you do," Frank said. "Look, your bartender doesn't know me."

"He made a mistake," the manager said.

"He doesn't know me and he never will."

"It's nothing, it's nothing," Alan said, waving his hands.

They sat at a table by the window. "I can't stand these out-of-work actors who think they're everybody's friend," Frank commented.

At dinner they talked about Nan Christie. Alan thought of her silk dresses, her devotion. The trouble, he said after a while, was that he never seemed to meet that kind of woman, the ones who sometimes walked by outside Jack's. The women he met were too human, he complained. Ever since his separation he'd been trying to find the right one.

"You shouldn't have any trouble," Frank said. "They're all looking for someone like you."

"They're looking for you."

"They think they are."

Frank paid the check without looking at it. "Once you've been married," Alan was explaining, "you want to be married again."

"I don't trust anyone enough to marry them," Frank said.

"What do you want then?"

"This is all right," Frank said.

Something was missing in him and women had always done anything to find out what it was. They always would. Perhaps it was simpler, Alan thought. Perhaps nothing was missing.

The car, which was a big Renault, a tourer, slowed down and pulled off the *autostrada* with Brenda asleep in back, her mouth a bit open and the daylight gleaming off her cheekbones. It was near Como, they had just crossed, the border police had glanced in at her.

"Come on, Bren, wake up," they said, "we're stopping for coffee."

She came back from the ladies' room with her hair combed and fresh lipstick on. The boy in the white jacket behind the counter was rinsing spoons.

"Hey, Brenda, I forget. Is it *espresso* or *expresso*?" Frank asked her.

"*Espresso*," she said.

"How do you know?"

"I'm from New York," she said.

"That's right," he remembered. "The Italians don't have an *x*, do they?"

"They don't have a *j* either," Alan said.

"Why is that?"

"They're such careless people," Brenda said. "They just lost them."

It was like old times. She was divorced from Doop or Boos or whoever. Her two little girls were with her mother. She had that quirky smile.

In Paris Frank had taken them to the Crazy Horse. In blackness like velvet the music struck up and six girls in unison kicked their legs in the brilliant light. They wore high heels and a little strapping. The nudity that is immortal. He was leaning on one elbow in the darkness. He glanced at Brenda. "Still studying, eh?" she said.

They were over for three weeks. Frank wasn't sure, maybe they would stay longer, take a house in the south of France or something. Their clients would have to struggle along without them. There comes a time, he said, when you have to get away for a while.

They had breakfast together in hotels with the sound of workmen chipping at the stone of the fountain outside. They listened to the angry woman shouting in the kitchen, drove to little towns, and drank every night. They had separate rooms, like staterooms, like passengers on a fading boat.

At noon the light shifted along the curve of buildings and people were walking far off. A wave of pigeons rose before a trotting dog. The man at the table in front of them had a pair of binoculars and was looking here and there. Two Swedish girls strolled past.

"Now they're turning dark," the man said.

"What is?" said his wife.

"The pigeons."

"Alan," Frank confided.

"What?"

"The pigeons are turning dark."

"That's too bad."

There was silence for a moment.

"Why don't you just take a photograph?" the woman said.

"A photograph?"

"Of those women. You're looking at them so much."

He put down the binoculars.

"You know, the curve is so graceful," she said. "It's what makes this square so perfect."

"Isn't the weather glorious?" Frank said in the same tone of voice.

"And the pigeons," Alan said.

"The pigeons, too."

After a while the couple got up and left. The pigeons leapt up for a running child and hissed overhead. "I see you're still playing games," Brenda said. Frank smiled.

"We ought to get together in New York," she said that evening. They were waiting for Alan to come down. She reached across the table to pick up a magazine. "You've never met my kids, have you?" she said.

"No."

"They're terrific kids." She leafed through the pages not paying attention to them. Her forearms were tanned. She was not wearing a wedding band. The first act was over or rather the first five minutes. Now came the plot. "Do you remember those nights at Goldie's?" she said.

"Things were different then, weren't they?"

"Not so different."

"What do you mean?"

She wiggled her bare third finger and glanced at him. Just then Alan appeared. He sat down and looked from one of them to the other. "What's wrong?" he asked. "Did I interrupt something?"

When the time came for her to leave she wanted them to drive to Rome. They could spend a couple of days and she would catch the plane. They weren't going that way, Frank said.

"It's only a three-hour drive."

"I know, but we're going the other way," he said.

"For God's sake. Why won't you drive me?"

"Let's do it," Alan said.

"Go ahead. I'll stay here."

"You should have gone into politics," Brenda said. "You have a real gift."

After she was gone the mood of things changed. They were by themselves. They drove through the sleepy country to the north. The green water slapped as darkness fell on Venice. The lights in some *palazzos* were on. On the curtained upper floors the legs of countesses uncoiled, slithering on the sheets like a serpent.

In Harry's, Frank held up a dense, icy glass and murmured his father's line, "Good night, nurse." He talked to some people at the next table, a German who was manager of a hotel in Düsseldorf and his girlfriend. She'd been looking at him. "Want a taste?" he asked her. It was his second. She drank looking directly at him. "Looks like you finished it," he said.

"Yes, I like to do that."

He smiled. When he was drinking he was strangely calm. In Lugano in the park that time a bird had sat on his shoe.

In the morning across the canal, wide as a river, the buildings of the Giudecca lay in their soft colors, a great sunken barge with roofs and the crowns of hidden trees. The first winds of autumn were blowing, ruffling the water.

Leaving Venice, Frank drove. He couldn't ride in a car unless he was driving. Alan sat back, looking out the window, sunlight falling on the hillsides of antiquity. European days, the silence, the needle floating at a hundred.

In Padua, Alan woke early. The stands were being set up in the market. It was before daylight and cool. A man was laying out boards on the pavement, eight of them like doors to set bags of grain on. He was wearing the jacket from a suit.

Searching in the truck he found some small pieces of wood and used them to shim the boards, testing with his foot.

The sky became violet. Under the colonnade the butchers had hung out chickens and roosters, spurred legs bound together. Two men sat trimming artichokes. The blue car of the *carabiniere* lazed past. The bags of rice and dry beans were set out now, the tops folded back like cuffs. A girl in a tailored coat with a scarf around her head called, "*Signore*," then arrogantly, "*dica!*"

He saw the world afresh, its pavements and architecture, the names that had lasted for a thousand years. It seemed that his life was being clarified, the sediment was drifting down. Across the street in a jeweler's shop a girl was laying things out in the window. She was wearing white gloves and arranging the pieces with great care. She glanced up as he stood watching. For a moment their eyes met, separated by the lighted glass. She was holding a lapis lazuli bracelet, the blue of the police car. Emboldened, he formed the silent words. *Quanto costa? Tre cento settante mille,* her lips said. It was eight in the morning when he got back to the hotel. A taxi pulled up and rattled the narrow street. A woman dressed for dinner got out and went inside.

The days passed. In Verona the points of the steeples and then its domes rose from the mist. The white-coated waiters appeared from the kitchen. *Primi, secondi, dolce.* They stopped in Arezzo. Frank came back to the table. He had some postcards. Alan was trying to write to his daughter once a week. He never knew what to say: where they were and what they'd seen. Giotto—what would that mean to her?

They sat in the car. Frank was wearing a soft tweed jacket.

It was like cashmere—he'd been shopping in Missoni and everywhere, windbreakers, shoes. Schoolgirls in dark skirts were coming through an arch across the street. After a while one came through alone. She stood as if waiting for someone. Alan was studying the map. He felt the engine start. Very slowly they moved forward. The window glided down.

"*Scusi, signorina,*" he heard Frank say.

She turned. She had pure features and her face was without expression, as if a bird had turned to look, a bird which might suddenly fly away.

Which way, Frank asked her, was the *centro*, the center of town? She looked one way and then the other. "There," she said.

"Are you sure?" he said. He turned his head unhurriedly to look more or less in the direction she was pointing.

"*Si,*" she said.

They were going to Siena, Frank said. There was silence. Did she know which road went to Siena?

She pointed the other way.

"Alan, you want to give her a ride?" he asked.

"What are you talking about?"

Two men in white smocks like doctors were working on the wooden doors of the church. They were up on top of some scaffolding. Frank reached back and opened the rear door.

"Do you want to go for a ride?" he asked. He made a little circular motion with his finger.

They drove through the streets in silence. The radio was playing. Nothing was said. Frank glanced at her in the rear-view mirror once or twice. It was at the time of a famous murder in Poland, the killing of a priest. Dusk was falling. The lights were coming on in shop windows and evening papers were in the kiosks. The body of the murdered man lay in a long coffin in the upper right corner of the *Corriere Della Sera*. It was in clean clothes like a worker after a terrible accident.

"Would you like an *aperitivo*?" Frank asked over his shoulder.

"*No*," she said.

They drove back to the church. He got out for a few minutes with her. His hair was very thin, Alan noticed. Strangely, it made him look younger. They stood talking, then she turned and walked down the street.

"What did you say to her?" Alan asked. He was nervous.

"I asked if she wanted a taxi."

"We're headed for trouble."

"There's not going to be any trouble," Frank said.

His room was on the corner. It was large, with a sitting area near the windows. On the wooden floor there were two worn oriental carpets. On a glass cabinet in the bathroom were his hairbrush, lotions, cologne. The towels were a pale green with the name of the hotel in white. She didn't look at any of that. He had given the *portiere* forty thousand lire. In Italy the laws were very strict. It was nearly the same hour of the afternoon. He kneeled to take off her shoes.

He had drawn the curtains but light came in around them. At one point she seemed to tremble, her body shuddered. "Are you all right?" he said.

She had closed her eyes.

Later, standing, he saw himself in the mirror. He seemed

to have thickened around the waist. He turned so that it was less noticeable. He got into bed again but was too hasty. "*Basta,*" she finally said.

They went down later and met Alan in a café. It was hard for him to look at them. He began to talk in a foolish way. What was she studying at school, he asked. For God's sake, Frank said. Well, what did her father do? She didn't understand.

"What work does he do?"

"Furniture," she said.

"He sells it?"

"*Restauro.*"

"In our country, no *restauro,*" Alan explained. He made a gesture. "Throw it away."

"I've got to start running again," Frank decided.

The next day was Saturday. He had the *portiere* call her number and hand him the phone.

"Hello, Eda? It's Frank."

"I know."

"What are you doing?"

He didn't understand her reply.

"We're going to Florence. You want to come to Florence?" he said. There was a silence. "Why don't you come and spend a few days?"

"No," she said.

"Why not?"

In a quieter voice she said, "How do I explain?"

"You can think of something."

At a table across the room children were playing cards while three well-dressed women, their mothers, sat and talked. There were cries of excitement as the cards were thrown down.

"Eda?"

She was still there. "*Si*," she said.

In the hills they were burning leaves. The smoke was invisible but they could smell it as they passed through, like the smell from a restaurant or paper mill. It made Frank suddenly remember childhood and country houses, raking the lawn with his father long ago. The green signs began to say Firenze. It started to rain. The wipers swept silently across the glass. Everything was beautiful and dim.

They had dinner in a restaurant of plain rooms, whitewashed, like vaults in a cellar. She looked very young. She looked like a young dog, the white of her eyes was that pure. She said very little and played with a strip of pink paper that had come off the menu.

In the morning they walked aimlessly. The windows displayed things for women who were older, in their thirties at least, silk dresses, bracelets, scarves. In Fendi's was a beautiful coat, the price beneath in small metal numbers.

"Do you like it?" he asked. "Come on, I'll buy it for you."

He wanted to see the coat in the window, he told them inside.

"For the *signorina*?"

"Yes."

She seemed uncomprehending. Her face was lost in the fur. He touched her cheek through it.

"You know how much that is?" Alan said. "Four million five hundred thousand."

"Do you like it?" Frank asked her.

She wore it continually. She watched the football matches on television in it, her legs curled beneath her. The room was in disorder, they hadn't been out all day.

"What do you say to leaving here?" Alan asked unexpectedly. The announcers were shouting in Italian. "I thought I'd like to see Spoleto."

"Sure. Where is it?" Frank said. He had his hand on her knee and was rubbing it with the barest movement, as one might a dozing cat.

The countryside was flat and misty. They were leaving the past behind them, unwashed glasses, towels on the bathroom floor. There was a stain on his lapel, Frank noticed in the dining room. He tried to get it off as the headwaiter grated fresh Parmesan over each plate. He dipped the corner of his napkin in water and rubbed the spot. The table was near the doorway, visible from the desk. Eda was fixing an earring.

"Cover it with your napkin," Alan told him.

"Here, get this off, will you?" he asked Eda.

She scratched at it quickly with her fingernail.

"What am I going to do without her?" Frank said.

"What do you mean, without her?"

"So this is Spoleto," he said. The spot was gone. "Let's have some more wine." He called the waiter. "*Senta.* Tell him," he said to Eda.

They laughed and talked about old times, the days when they were getting eight hundred dollars a week and working ten, twelve hours a day. They remembered Weyland and the veins in his nose. The word he always used was "vivid," testimony a bit too vivid, far too vivid, a rather vivid decor.

They left talking loudly. Eda was close between them in

her huge coat. "*Alla rovina*," the clerk at the front desk muttered as they reached the street, "*alle macerie*," he said, the girl at the switchboard looked over at him, "*alla polvere*." It was something about rubbish and dust.

The mornings grew cold. In the garden there were leaves piled against the table legs. Alan sat alone in the bar. A waitress, the one with the mole on her lip, came in and began to work the coffee machine. Frank came down. He had an overcoat across his shoulders. In his shirt without a tie he looked like a rich patient in some hospital. He looked like a man who owned a produce business and had been playing cards all night.

"So, what do you think?" Alan said.

Frank sat down. "Beautiful day," he commented. "Maybe we ought to go somewhere."

In the room, perhaps in the entire hotel, their voices were the only sound, irregular and low, like the soft strokes of someone sweeping. One muted sound, then another.

"Where's Eda?"

"She's taking a bath."

"I thought I'd say good-bye to her."

"Why? What's wrong?"

"I think I'm going home."

"What happened?" Frank said.

Alan could see himself in the mirror behind the bar, his sandy hair. He looked pale somehow, nonexistent. "Nothing happened," he said. She had come into the bar and was sitting at the other end of the room. He felt a tightness in his chest. "Europe depresses me."

Frank was looking at him. "Is it Eda?"

"No. I don't know." It seemed terribly quiet. Alan put his hands in his lap. They were trembling.

"Is that all it is? We can share her," Frank said.

"What do you mean?" He was too nervous to say it right. He stole a glance at Eda. She was looking at something outside in the garden.

"Eda," Frank called, "do you want something to drink? *Cosa vuoi?*" He made a motion of glass raised to the mouth. In college he had been a great favorite. Shuford had been shortened to Shuf and then Shoes. He had run in the Penn Relays. His mother could trace her family back for six generations.

"Orange juice," she said.

They sat there talking quietly. That was often the case, Eda had noticed. They talked about business or things in New York.

When they came back to the hotel that night, Frank explained it. She understood in an instant. No. She shook her head. Alan was sitting alone in the bar. He was drinking some kind of sweet liqueur. It wouldn't happen, he knew. It didn't matter anyway. Still, he felt shamed. The hotel above his head, its corridors and quiet rooms, what else were they for?

Frank and Eda came in. He managed to turn to them. She seemed impassive—he could not tell. What was this he was drinking, he finally asked? She didn't understand the question. He saw Frank nod once slightly, as if in agreement. They were like thieves.

In the morning the first light was blue on the window glass. There was the sound of rain. It was leaves blowing in the garden, shifting across the gravel. Alan slipped from the bed to fasten the loose shutter. Below, half hidden in the hedges, a statue gleamed white. The few parked cars shone faintly. She was asleep, the soft, heavy pillow beneath her head. He was afraid to wake her. "Eda," he whispered, "Eda."

Her eyes opened a bit and closed. She was young and could stay asleep. He was afraid to touch her. She was unhappy, he knew, her bare neck, her hair, things he could not see. It would be a while before they were used to it. He didn't know what to do. Apart from that, it was perfect. It was the most natural thing in the world. He would buy her something himself, something beautiful.

In the bathroom he lingered at the window. He was thinking of the first day they had come to work at Weyland, Braun—he and Frank. They would become inseparable. Autumn in the gardens of the Veneto. It was barely dawn. He would always remember meeting Frank. He couldn't have done these things himself. A young man in a cap suddenly came out of a doorway below. He crossed the driveway and jumped onto a motorbike. The engine started, a faint blur. The headlight appeared and off he went, delivery basket in back. He was going to get the rolls for breakfast. His life was simple. The air was pure and cool. He was part of that great, unchanging order of those who live by wages, whose world is unlit and who do not realize what is above.

FOREIGN SHORES

Mrs. Pence and her white shoes were gone. She had left two days before, and the room at the top of the stairs was empty, cosmetics no longer littering the dresser, the ironing board finally taken down. Only a few scattered hairpins and a dusting of talcum remained. The next day Truus came with two suitcases and splotched cheeks. It was March and cold. Christopher met her in the kitchen as if by accident. "Do you shoot people?" he asked.

She was Dutch and had no work permit, it turned out. The house was a mess. "I can pay you 135 dollars a week," Gloria told her.

Christopher didn't like her at first, but soon the dishes piled on the counter were washed and put away, the floor was swept, and things were more or less returned to order—the cleaning girl came only once a week. Truus was slow but diligent. She did the laundry, which Mrs. Pence who was a registered nurse had always refused to do, shopped, cooked meals, and took care of Christopher. She was a hard worker, nineteen, and in sulky bloom. Gloria sent her to Elizabeth Arden's in Southampton to get her complexion cleared up and gave her Mondays and one night a week off.

Gradually Truus learned about things. The house, which was a large, converted carriage house, was rented. Gloria, who was twenty-nine, liked to sleep late, and burned spots sometimes appeared in the living room rug. Christopher's father lived in California, and Gloria had a boyfriend named Ned. "That son of a bitch," she often said, "might as well forget about seeing Christopher again until he pays me what he owes me."

"Absolutely," Ned said.

When the weather became warmer Truus could be seen in the village in one shop or another or walking along the street with Christopher in tow. She was somewhat drab. She had met another girl by then, a French girl, also an *au pair*, with whom she went to the movies. Beneath the trees with their new leaves the expensive cars glided along, more of them every week. Truus began taking Christopher to the beach. Gloria watched them go off. She was often still in her bathrobe. She waved and drank coffee. She was very lucky. All her friends told her and she knew it herself: Truus was a prize. She had made herself part of the family.

"Truus knows where to get pet mices," Christopher said.

"To get what?"

"Little mices."

"Mice," Gloria said.

He was watching her apply makeup, which fascinated him. Face nearly touching the mirror, intent, she stroked her long lashes upward. She had a great mass of blonde hair, a mole on her upper lip with a few untouched hairs growing from it, a small blemish on her forehead, but otherwise a beautiful face. Her first entrance was always stunning. Later you might notice the thin legs, aristocratic legs she called them, her mother had them, too. As the evening wore on her perfection diminished. The gloss disappeared from her lips, she misplaced earrings. The highway patrol all knew her. A few weeks before she had driven into a ditch on the way home from a party and walked down Georgica Road at three in the morning, breaking two panes of glass to get in the kitchen door.

"Her friend knows where to get them," Christopher said.

"Which friend?"

"Oh, just a friend," Truus said.

"We met him."

Gloria's eyes shifted from their own reflection to rest for a moment on that of Truus who was watching, no less absorbed.

"Can I have some mices?" Christopher pleaded.

"Hmm?"

"Please."

"No, darling."

"Please!"

"No, we have enough of our own as it is."

"Where?"

"All over the house."

"Please!"

"No. Now stop it." To Truus she remarked casually, "Is it a boyfriend?"

"It's no one," Truus said. "Just someone I met."

"Well, just remember you have to watch yourself. You never know who you're meeting, you have to be careful." She drew back slightly and examined her eyes, large and black-rimmed. "Just thank God you're not in Italy," she said.

"Italy?"

"You can't even walk out on the street there. You can't even buy a pair of shoes, they're all over you, touching and pawing."

It happened outside Dean and De Luca's when Christopher insisted on carrying the bag and just past the door had dropped it.

"Oh, look at that," Truus said in irritation. "I told you not to drop it."

"I didn't drop it. It slipped."

"Don't touch it," she warned. "There's broken glass."

Christopher stared at the ground. He had a sturdy body, bobbed hair, and a cleft in his chin like his banished father's. People were walking past them. Truus was annoyed. It was hot, the store was crowded, she would have to go back inside.

"Looks like you had a little accident," a voice said. "Here, what'd you break? That's all right, they'll exchange it. I know the cashier."

When he came out again a few moments later he said to Christopher, "Think you can hold it this time?"

Christopher was silent.

"What's your name?"

"Well, tell him," Truus said. Then after a moment, "His name is Christopher."

"Too bad you weren't with me this morning, Christopher.

I went to a place where they had a lot of tame mice. Ever seen any?"

"Where?" Christopher said.

"They sit right in your hand."

"Where is it?"

"You can't have a mouse," Truus said.

"Yes, I can." He continued to repeat it as they walked along. "I can have anything I want," he said.

"Be quiet." They were talking above his head. Near the corner they stopped for a while. Christopher was silent as they went on talking. He felt his hair being tugged but did not look up.

"Say good-bye, Christopher."

He said nothing. He refused to lift his head.

In midafternoon the sun was like a furnace. Everything was dark against it, the horizon lost in haze. Far down the beach in front of one of the prominent houses a large flag was waving. With Christopher following her, Truus trudged through the sand. Finally she saw what she had been looking for. Up in the dunes a figure was sitting.

"Where are we going?" Christopher asked.

"Just up here."

Christopher soon saw where they were headed.

"I have mices," was the first thing he said.

"Is that right?"

"Do you want to know their names?" In fact they were two desperate gerbils in a tank of wood shavings. "Catman and Batty," he said.

"Catman?"

"He's the big one." Truus was spreading a towel, he noticed. "Do we have to stay here?"

"Yes."

"Why?" he asked. He wanted to go down near the water. Finally Truus agreed.

"But only if you stay where I can see you," she said.

The shovel fell out of his bucket as he ran off. She had to call him to make him come back. He went off again and she pretended to watch him.

"I'm really glad you came. You know, I don't know your name. I know his, but I don't know yours."

"Truus."

"I've never heard that name before. What is it, French?"

"It's Dutch."

"Oh, yeah?"

His name was Robbie Werner, "not half as nice," he said. He had an easy smile and pale blue eyes. There was something spoiled about him, like a student who has been expelled and is undisturbed by it. The sun was roaring down and striking Truus' shoulders beneath her shirt. She was wearing a blue one-piece bathing suit underneath. She was aware of being too heavy, of the heat, and of the thick, masculine legs stretched out near her.

"Do you live here?" she said.

"I'm just here on vacation."

"From where?"

"Try and guess."

"I don't know," she said. She wasn't good at that kind of thing.

"Saudi Arabia," he said. "It's about three times this hot."

He worked there, he explained. He had an apartment of his own and a free telephone. At first she did not believe him. She glanced at him as he talked and realized he was telling the truth. He got two months of vacation a year, he said, usually in Europe. She imagined it as sleeping in hotels and getting up late and going out to lunch. She did not want him to stop talking. She could not think of anything to say.

"How about you?" he said. "What do you do?"

"Oh, I'm just taking care of Christopher."

"Where's his mother?"

"She lives here. She's divorced," Truus said.

"It's terrible the way people get divorced," he said.

"I agree with you."

"I mean, why get married?" he said. "Are your parents still married?"

"Yes," she said, although they did not seem to be a good example. They had been married for nearly twenty-five years. They were worn out from marriage, her mother especially.

Suddenly Robbie raised himself slightly. "Uh-oh," he said.

"What is it?"

"Your kid. I don't see him."

Truus jumped up quickly, looked around, and began to run toward the water. There was a kind of shelf the tide had made which hid the ocean's edge. As she ran she finally saw, beyond it, the little blond head. She was calling his name.

"I told you to stay up where I could see you," she cried, out of breath, when she reached him. "I had to run all the way. Do you know how much you frightened me?"

Christopher slapped aimlessly at the sand with his shovel. He looked up and saw Robbie. "Do you want to build a castle?" he asked innocently.

"Sure," Robbie said after a moment. "Come on, let's go down a little further, closer to the water. Then we can have a moat. Do you want to help us build a castle?" he said to Truus.

"No," Christopher said, "she can't."

"Sure, she can. She's going to do a very important part of it for us."

"What?"

"You'll see." They were walking down the velvety slope dampened by the tide.

"What's your name?" Christopher asked.

"Robbie. Here's a good place." He kneeled and began scooping out large handfuls of sand.

"Do you have a penis?"

"Sure."

"I do, too," Christopher said.

She was preparing his dinner while he played outside on the terrace, banging on the slate with his shovel. It was hot. Her clothes were sticking to her and there was moisture on her upper lip, but afterward she would go up and shower. She had a room on the second floor—not the one Mrs. Pence had—a small guest room painted white with a crude patch on the door where the original lock had been removed. Just outside the window were trees and the thick hedge of the neighboring house. The room faced south and caught the breeze. Often in the morning Christopher would crawl into her bed, his legs cool and hair a little sour-smelling. The room was filled with molten light. She could feel sand in the sheets, the merest trace of it. She turned her head sleepily to look at her watch on the night table. Not yet six. The first birds were singing. Beside her, eyes closed, mouth parted to reveal a row of small teeth, lay this perfect boy.

He had begun digging in the border of flowers. He was piling dirt on the edge of the terrace.

"Don't, you'll hurt them," Truus said. "If you don't stop, I'm going to put you up in the tree, the one by the shed."

The telephone was ringing. Gloria picked it up in the other part of the house. After a moment, "It's for you," she called.

"Hello?" Truus said.

"Hi." It was Robbie.

"Hello," she said. She couldn't tell if Gloria had hung up. Then she heard a click.

"Are you going to be able to meet me tonight?"

"Yes, I can meet you," she said. Her heart felt extraordinarily light.

Christopher had begun to scrape his shovel across the screen. "Excuse me," she said, putting her hand over the mouthpiece. "Stop that," she commanded.

She turned to him after she hung up. He was watching from the door. "Are you hungry?" she asked.

"No."

"Come, let's wash your hands."

"Why are you going out?"

"Just for fun. Come on."

"Where are you going?"

"Oh, stop, will you?"

That night the air was still. The heat spread over one immediately, like a flush. In the thunderous cool of the Laundry,
past the darkened station, they sat near the bar which was
lined with men. It was noisy and crowded. Every so often
someone passing by would say hello.

"Some zoo, huh?" Robbie said.

Gloria came there often, she knew.

"What do you want to drink?"

"Beer," she said.

There were at least twenty men at the bar. She was aware
of occasional glances.

"You know, you don't look bad in a bathing suit," Robbie
said.

The opposite, she felt, was true.

"Have you ever thought of taking off a few pounds?" he
said. He had a calm, unhurried way of speaking. "It could
really help you."

"Yes, I know," she said.

"Have you ever thought of modeling?"

She would not look at him.

"I'm serious," he said. "You have a nice face."

"I'm not quite a model," she murmured.

"That's not the only thing. You also have a very nice ass,
you don't mind me saying that?"

She shook her head.

Later they drove past large, dark houses and down a road

which unexpectedly opened at the end like the vista she knew was somehow opening to her. There were gently rolling fields and distant lights. A street sign saying Egypt Lane—she was too dizzy to read it—floated for an instant in the headlights.

"Do you know where we are?"

"No," she said.

"That's the Maidstone Club."

They crossed a small bridge and went on. Finally they turned into a driveway. She could hear the ocean when he shut off the ignition. There were two other cars parked nearby.

"Is someone here?"

"No, they're all asleep," he whispered.

They walked on the grass to the other side of the house. His room was in a kind of annex. There was a smell of dampness. The dresser was strewn with clothes, shaving gear, magazines. She saw all this vaguely when he struck a match to light a candle.

"Are you sure no one's here?" she said.

"Don't worry."

It was all a little clumsy. Afterward they showered together.

There was almost nothing on the menu Gloria was interested in eating.

"What are you going to have?" she said.

"Crab salad," Ned said.

"I think I'll have the avocado," she decided.

The waiter took the menus.

"A pharmaceutical company, you say?"

"I think he works for some big one," she said.

"Which one?"

"I don't know. It's in Saudi Arabia."

"Saudi Arabia?" he said doubtfully.

"That's where all the money is, isn't it?" she said. "It certainly isn't here."

"How'd she meet this fellow?"

"Picked him up, I think."

"Typical," he said. He pushed his rimless glasses higher on his nose with one finger. He was wearing a string sweater with the sleeves pulled up. His hair was faded by the sun. He looked very boyish and handsome. He was thirty-three and had never been married. There were only two things wrong with him: his mother had all the money in a trust, and his back. Something was wrong with it. He had terrible spasms and sometimes had to lie for hours on the floor.

"Well, I'm sure he knows she's just a baby-sitter. He's here on vacation. I hope he doesn't break her heart," Gloria said. "Actually, I'm glad he showed up. It's better for Christopher. She's less likely to return the erotic feelings he has for her."

"The what?"

"Believe me, I'm not imagining it."

"Oh, come on, Gloria."

"There's something going on. Maybe she doesn't know it. He's in her bed all the time."

"He's only five."

"They can have erections at five," Gloria said.

"Oh, really."

"Darling, I've seen him with them."

"At five?"

"You'd be surprised," she said. "They're born with them. You just don't remember, that's all."

She did not become lovesick, she did not brood. She was more silent in the weeks that followed but also more settled, not particularly sad. In the flat-heeled shoes which gave her a slightly dumpy appearance she went shopping as usual. The thought even crossed Gloria's mind that she might be pregnant.

"Is everything all right?" she asked.

"Pardon?"

"Darling, do you feel all right? You know what I mean."

There were times when the two of them came back from the beach and Truus patiently brushed the sand from Christopher's feet that Gloria felt great sympathy for her and understood why she was quiet. How much of fate lay in one's appearance! Truus' face seemed empty, without expression, except when she was playing with Christopher and then it brightened. She was so like a child anyway, a bulky child, an unimaginative playmate who in the course of things would be forgotten. And the foolishness of her dreams! She wanted to become a fashion designer, she said one day. She was interested in designing clothes.

What she actually felt after her boyfriend left, no one knew. She came in carrying the groceries, the screen door banged behind her. She answered the phone, took messages. In the evening she sat on the worn couch with Christopher watching television upstairs. Sometimes they both laughed. The shelves were piled with games, plastic toys, children's books. Once in a while Christopher was told to bring one down so his mother could read him a story. It was very important that he like books, Gloria said.

It was a pale blue envelope with Arabic printing in the corner. Truus opened it standing at the kitchen counter and began to read the letter. The handwriting was childish and small. *Dear Truus*, it said. *Thank you for your letter. I was glad to receive it. You don't have to put so many stamps on letters to Saudi Arabia though. One U.S. airmail is enough. I'm glad to hear you miss me.* She looked up. Christopher was banging on something in the doorway.

"This won't work," he said.

He was dragging a toy car that had to be pumped with air to run.

"Here, let me see," she said. He seemed on the verge of tears. "This fits here, doesn't it?" She attached the small plastic hose. "There, now it will work."

"No, it won't," he said.

"No, it won't," she mimicked.

He watched gloomily as she pumped. When the handle grew stiff she put the car on the floor, pointed it, and let it go. It leapt across the room and crashed into the opposite wall. He went over and nudged it with his foot.

"Do you want to play with it?"

"No."

"Then pick it up and put it away."

He didn't move.

"Put . . . it . . . away . . ." she said, in a deep voice, coming toward him one step at a time. He watched from the corner of his eye. Another tottering step. "Or I eat you," she growled.

He ran for the stairs shrieking. She continued to chant, shuffling slowly toward the stairs. The dog was barking. Gloria came in the door, reaching down to pull off her shoes and kick them to one side. "Hi, any calls?" she asked.

Truus abandoned her performance. "No. No one."

Gloria had been visiting her mother, which was always tiresome. She looked around. Something was going on, she realized. "Where's Christopher?"

A glint of blond hair appeared above the landing.

"Hello, darling," she said. There was a pause. "Mummy said hello. What's wrong? What's happening?"

"We're just playing a game," Truus explained.

"Well, stop playing for a moment and come and kiss me."

She took him into the living room. Truus went upstairs. Sometime later she heard her name being called. She folded the letter which she had read for the fifth or sixth time and went to the head of the stairs. "Yes?"

"Can you come down?" Gloria called. "He's driving me crazy."

"He's impossible," she said, when Truus arrived. "He spilled his milk, he's kicked over the dog water. Look at this mess!"

"Let's go outside and play a game," Truus said to him, reaching for his hand which he pulled away. "Come. Or do you want to go on the pony?"

He stared at the floor. As if she were alone in the room

she got down on her hands and knees. She shook her hair loose and made a curious sound, a faint neigh, pure as the tinkle of glass. She turned to gaze indifferently at him over her shoulder. He was watching.

"Come," she said calmly. "Your pony is waiting."

After that when the letters arrived, Truus would fold them and slip them into her pocket while Gloria went through the mail: bills, gallery openings, urgent requests for payment, occasionally a letter. She wrote very few herself but always complained when she did not receive them. Comments on the logic of this only served to annoy her.

The fall was coming. Everything seemed to deny it. The days were still warm, the great, terminal sun poured down. The leaves, more luxuriant than ever, covered the trees. Behind the hedges, lawn mowers made a final racket. On the warm slate of the terrace, left behind, a grasshopper, a veteran in dark green and yellow, limped along. The birds had torn off one of his legs.

One morning Gloria was upstairs when something happened to catch her eye. The door to the little guest room was open and on the night table, folded, was a letter. It lay there in the silence, half of it raised like a wing in the air. The house was empty. Truus had gone to shop and pick up Christopher at nursery school. With the curiosity of a schoolgirl, Gloria sat down on the bed. She unfolded the envelope and took out the pages. The first thing her eye fell upon was a line just above the middle. It stunned her. For a moment she was dazed. She read the letter through nervously. She opened the drawer. There were others. She read them as well. Like love letters they were repetitious, but they were not love letters. He did more than work in an office, this man, much more. He went through Europe, city after city, looking for young people who in hotel rooms and cheap apartments— she was horrified by her images of it—stripped and were immersed in a river of sordid acts. The letters were like those of a high school boy, that was the most terrible part. They were letters of recruitment, so simple they might have been copied out by an illiterate.

Sitting there framed in the doorway, her hand nearly trembling, she could not think of what to do. She felt deeply upset, frightened, betrayed. She glanced out the window. She wondered if she should go immediately to the nursery school —she could be there in minutes—and take Christopher somewhere where he would be safe. No, that would be fool-ish. She hurried downstairs to the telephone.

"Ned," she said when she reached him—her voice was shaking. She was looking at one of the letters which asked a number of matter-of-fact questions.

"What is it? Is anything wrong?"

"Come right away. I need you. Something's happened."

For a while then she stood there with the letters in her hand. Looking around hurriedly, she put them in a drawer where garden seeds were kept. She began to calculate how long it would be before he would be there, driving out from the city.

She heard them come in. She was in her bedroom. She had regained her composure, but as she entered the kitchen she could feel her heart beating wildly. Truus was preparing lunch.

"Mummy, look at this," Christopher said. He held up a sheet of paper. "Do you see what this is?"

"Yes. It's very nice."

"This is the engine," he said. "These are the wings. These are the guns."

She tried to focus her attention on the scrawled outline with its garish colors, but she was conscious only of the girl at work behind the counter. As Truus brought the plates to the table, Gloria tried to look calmly at her face, a face she realized she had not seen before. In it she recognized for the first time depravity, and in Truus' limbs, their smoothness, their volume, she saw brutality and vice. Outside, in the ordinary daylight, were the trees along the side of the property, the roof of a house, the lawn, some scattered toys. It was a landscape that seemed ominous, too idyllic, too still.

"Don't use your fingers, Christopher," Truus said, sitting down with him. "Use your fork."

"It won't reach," he said.

She pushed the plate an inch or two toward him.

"Here, try now," she said.

Later, watching them play outside on the grass, Gloria could not help noticing a wild, almost a bestial aspect in her son's excitement, as if a crudeness were somehow becoming part of him, soiling him. A line from the many that lay writhing in her head came forth. *I hope you will be ready to take my big cock when I see you again. P.S. Have you had any big cocks lately? I miss you and think of you and it makes me very hard.* "Have you ever read anything like that?" Gloria asked.

"Not exactly."

"It's the most disgusting thing. I can't believe it."

"Of course, she didn't write them," Ned said.

"She kept them, that's worse."

He had them all in his hand. *If you came to Europe it would be great*, one said. *We would travel and you could help me. We could work together. I know you would be very good at it. The girls we would be looking for are between 13 and 18 years old. Also guys, a little older.*

"You have to go in there and tell her to leave," Gloria said. "Tell her she has to be out of the house."

He looked at the letters again. *Some of them are very well developed, you would be surprised. I think you know the type we are looking for.*

"I don't know . . . Maybe these are just a silly kind of love letter."

"Ned, I'm not kidding," she said.

Of course, there would be a lot of fucking, too.

"I'm going to call the FBI."

"No," he said, "that's all right. Here, take these. I'll go and tell her."

Truus was in the kitchen. As he spoke to her he tried to see in her grey eyes the boldness he had overlooked. There was only confusion. She did not seem to understand him. She went in to Gloria. She was nearly in tears. "But why?" she wanted to know.

"I found the letters," was all Gloria would say.

"What letters?"

They were lying on the desk. Gloria picked them up.

"They're mine," Truus protested. "They belong to me."

"I've called the FBI," Gloria said.

"Please, give them to me."

"I'm not giving them to you. I'm burning them."

"Please let me have them," Truus insisted.

She was confused and weeping. She passed Ned on her way upstairs. He thought he could see the attributes praised in the letters, the Saudi letters, as he later called them.

In her room Truus sat on the bed. She did not know what she would do or where she would go. She began to pack her clothes, hoping that somehow things might change if she took long enough. She moved very slowly.

"Where are you going?" Christopher said from the door.

She did not answer him. He asked again, coming into the room.

"I'm going to see my mother," she said.

"She's downstairs."

Truus shook her head.

"Yes, she is," he insisted.

"Go away. Don't bother me right now," she said in a flat voice.

He began kicking at the door with his foot. After a while he sat on the couch. Then he disappeared.

When the taxi came for her, he was hiding behind some trees out near the driveway. She had been looking for him at the end.

"Oh, there you are," she said. She put down her suitcases and kneeled to say good-bye. He stood with his head bent. From a distance it seemed a kind of submission.

"Look at that," Gloria said. She was in the house. Ned was standing behind her. "They always love sluts," she said.

Christopher stood beside the road after the taxi had gone. That night he came down to his mother's room. He was crying and she turned on the light.

"What is it?" she said. She tried to comfort him. "Don't cry, darling. Did something frighten you? Here, mummy will take you upstairs. Don't worry. Everything will be all right."

"Good night, Christopher," Ned said.

"Say good night, darling."

She went up, climbed into bed with him, and finally got him to sleep, but he kicked so much she came back down, holding her robe closed with her hand. Ned had left her a note: his back was giving him trouble, he had gone home.

Truus' place was taken by a Colombian woman who was very religious and did not drink or smoke. Then by a black girl named Mattie who did both but stayed for a long time.

One night in bed, reading *Town and Country*, Gloria came across something that stunned her. It was a photograph of a garden party in Brussels, only a small photograph but she recognized a face, she was absolutely certain of it, and with a terrible sinking feeling she moved the page closer to the light. She was without makeup and at her most vulnerable. She examined the picture closely. She was no longer talking to Ned, she hadn't seen him for over a year, but she was tempted to call him anyway. Then, reading the caption and looking at the picture again she decided she was mistaken. It wasn't Truus, just someone who resembled her, and anyway what did it matter? It all seemed long ago. Christopher had forgotten about her. He was in school now, doing very well, on the soccer team already, playing with eight- and nine-year-olds, bigger than them and bright. He would be six three. He would have girlfriends hanging all over him, girls whose families had houses in the Bahamas. He would devastate them.

Still, lying there with the magazine on her knees she could not help thinking of it. What had actually become of Truus? She looked at the photograph again. Had she found her way to Amsterdam or Paris and, making dirty movies or whatever, met someone? It was unbearable to think of her being invited to places, slimmer now, sitting in the brilliance of crowded restaurants with her complexion still bad beneath the makeup and the morals of a housefly. The idea that there is an unearned happiness, that certain people find their way to it, nearly made her sick. Like the girl Ned was marrying who used to work in the catering shop just off the highway near Bridgehampton. That had been a blow, that had been more than a blow. But then nothing, almost nothing, really made sense anymore.

THE CINEMA

I.

At ten-thirty then, she arrived. They were waiting. The door at the far end opened and somewhat shyly, trying to see in the dimness if anyone was there, her long hair hanging like a schoolgirl's, everyone watching, she slowly, almost reluctantly approached. . . . Behind her came the young woman who was her secretary.

Great faces cannot be explained. She had a long nose, a mouth, a curious distance between the eyes. It was a face open and unknowable. It pronounced itself somehow indifferent to life.

When he was introduced to her, Guivi, the leading man, smiled. His teeth were large and there existed a space between the incisors. On his chin was a mole. These defects at that time were revered. He'd had only four or five roles, his discovery was sudden, the shot in which he appeared for the first time was often called one of the most memorable introductions in all of film. It was true. There is sometimes one image which outlasts everything, even the names are forgotten. He held her chair. She acknowledged the introductions faintly, one could hardly hear her voice.

The director leaned forward and began to talk. They would

rehearse for ten days in this bare hall. Anna's face was buried in her collar as he spoke. The director was new to her. He was a small man known as a hard worker. The saliva flew from his mouth as he talked. She had never rehearsed a film before, not for Fellini, not for Chabrol. She was trying to listen to what he said. She felt strongly the presence of others around her. Guivi sat calmly, smoking a cigarette. She glanced at him unseen.

They began to read, sitting at the table together. Make no attempt to find meaning, Iles told them, not so soon, this was only the first step. There were no windows. There was neither day nor night. Their words seemed to rise, to vanish like smoke above them. Guivi read his lines as if laying down cards of no particular importance. Bridge was his passion. He gave it all his nights. Halfway through, he touched her shoulder lightly as he was doing an intimate part. She seemed not to notice. She was like a lizard, only her throat was beating. The next time he touched her hair. That single gesture, so natural as to be almost unintended, made her quiet, stilled her fears.

She fled afterward. She went directly back to the Hotel de Ville. Her room was filled with objects. On the desk were books still wrapped in brown paper, magazines in various languages, letters hastily read. There was a small anteroom, not regularly shaped, and a bedroom beyond. The bed was large. In the manner of a sequence when the camera carefully, increasing our apprehension, moves from detail to detail, the bathroom door, half-open, revealed a vast array of bottles, of dark perfumes, medicines, things unknown. Far below on Via Sistina was the sound of traffic.

The next day she was better, she was like a woman ready to work. She brushed her hair back with her hand as she read. She was attentive, once she even laughed.

They were brought small cups of coffee from across the courtyard.

"How does it sound to you?" she asked the writer.

"Well . . ." he hesitated.

He was a wavering man named Peter Lang, at one time Lengsner. He had seen her in all her sacred life, a figure of lights, he had read the article, the love letter written to her in *Bazaar*. It described her perfect modesty, her instinct, the shape of her face. On the opposite page was the photograph he cut out and placed in his journal. This film he had written, this important work of the newest of the arts, already existed complete in his mind. Its power came from its chasteness, the discipline of its images. It was a film of indirection, the surface was calm with the calm of daily life. That was not to say still. Beneath the visible were emotions more potent for their concealment. Only occasionally, like the head of an iceberg ominously rising from nowhere and then dropping from sight did the terror come into view.

When she turned to him then, he was overwhelmed, he couldn't think of what to say. It didn't matter. Guivi gave an answer.

"I think we're still a little afraid of some of the lines," he said. "You know, you've written some difficult things."

"Ah, well . . ."

"Almost impossible. Don't misunderstand, they're good, except they have to be perfectly done."

She had already turned away and was talking to the director.

"Shakespeare is filled with lines like this," Guivi continued. He began to quote Othello.

It was now Iles' turn, the time to expose his ideas. He plunged in. He was like a kind of crazy schoolmaster as he described the work, part Freud, part lovelorn columnist, tracing interior lines and motives deep as rivers. Members of the crew had sneaked in to stand near the door. Guivi jotted something in his script.

"Yes, notes, make notes," Iles told him, "I am saying some brilliant things."

A performance was built up in layers, like a painting, that was his method, to start with this, add this, then this, and so forth. It expanded, became rich, developed depths and undercurrents. Then in the end they would cut it back, reduce it to half its size. That was what he meant by good acting.

He confided to Lang, "I never tell them everything. I'll give you an example: the scene in the clinic. I tell Guivi he's going to pieces, he thinks he's going to scream, actually scream. He has to stuff a towel in his mouth to prevent it. Then, just before we shoot, I tell him: Do it without the towel. Do you see?"

His energy began to infect the performers. A mood of excitement, even fever came over them. He was thrilling them, it was their world he was describing and then taking to pieces to reveal its marvelous intricacies.

If he was a genius, he would be crowned in the end because, like Balzac, his work was so vast. He, too, was filling page after page, unending, crowded with the sublime and the ordinary, fantastic characters, insights, human frailty, trash. If I make two films a year for thirty years, he said . . . The project was his life.

At six the limousines were waiting. The sky still had light, the cold of autumn was in the air. They stood near the door and talked. They parted reluctantly. He had converted them, he was their master. They drove off separately with a little wave. Lang was left standing in the dusk.

There were dinners. Guivi sat with Anna beside him. It was the fourth day. She leaned her head against his shoulder. He was discussing the foolishness of women. They were not genuinely intelligent, he said, that was a myth of Western society.

"I'm going to surprise you," Iles said, "do you know what I believe? I believe they're not as intelligent as men. They are *more* intelligent."

Anna shook her head very slightly.

"They're not logical," Guivi said. "It's not their way. A woman's whole essence is here." He indicated down near his stomach. "The womb," he said. "Nowhere else. Do you realize there are no great women bridge players?"

It was as if she had submitted to all his ideas. She ate without speaking. She barely touched dessert. She was content to be what he admired in a woman. She was aware of her power, he knelt to it nightly, his mind wandering. He was already becoming indifferent to her. He performed the act as one plays a losing hand, he did the best he could with it. The cloud of white leapt from him. She moaned.

"I am really a romantic and a classicist," he said. "I have *almost* been in love twice."

Her glance fell, he told her something in a whisper.

"But never really," he said, "never deeply. No, I long for that. I am ready for it."

Beneath the table her hand discovered this. The waiters were brushing away the crumbs.

Lang was staying at the Inghilterra in a small room on the side. Long after the evening was over he still swam in thoughts of it. He washed his underwear distractedly. Somewhere in the shuttered city, the river black with fall, he knew they were together, he did not resent it. He lay in bed like a poor student—how little life changes from the first to the last—and fell asleep clutching his dreams. The windows were open. The cold air poured over him like sea on a blind sailor, drenching him, filling the room. He lay with his legs crossed at the ankle like a martyr, his face turned to God.

Iles was at the Grand in a suite with tall doors and floors that creaked. He could hear chambermaids pass in the hall. He had a cold and could not sleep. He called his wife in America, it was just evening there, and they talked for a long time. He was depressed: Guivi was no actor.

"What's wrong with him?"

"Oh, he has nothing, no depth, no emotion."

"Can't you get someone else?"

"It's too late."

They would have to work around it, he said. He had the telephone propped on the pillow, his eyes were drifting aimlessly around the room. They would have to change the character somehow, make the falseness a part of it. Anna was all right. He was pleased with Anna. Well, they would do something, pump life into it somehow, make dead birds fly.

By the end of the week they were rehearsing on their feet. It was cold. They wore their coats as they moved from one place to another. Anna stood near Guivi. She took the cigarette from his fingers and smoked it. Sometimes they laughed.

Iles was alive with work. His hair fell in his face, he was explaining actions, details. He didn't rely on their knowledge, he arranged it all. Often he tied a line to an action, that is to say the words were keyed by it: Guivi touched Anna's elbow, without looking she said, "Go away."

Lang sat and watched. Sometimes they were working very close to him, just in front of where he was. He couldn't really pay attention. She was speaking *his* lines, things he had invented. They were like shoes. She tried them on, they were nice, she never thought who had made them.

"Anna has a limited range," Guivi confided.

Lang said yes. He wanted to learn more about acting, this secret world.

"But what a face," Guivi said.

"Her eyes!"

"There is a little touch of the idiot in them, isn't there?" Guivi said.

She could see them talking. Afterward she sent someone to Lang. Whatever he had told Guivi, she wanted to know, too. Lang looked over at her. She was ignoring him.

He was confused, he did not know if it was serious. The minor actors with nothing to do were sitting on two old sofas. The floor was chalky, dust covered their shoes. Iles was following the scenes closely, nodding his approval, yes, yes, good, excellent. The script girl walked behind him, a stopwatch around her neck. She was forty-five, her legs ached at night. She went along noting everything, careful not to step on any of the half-driven nails.

"My love," Iles turned to her, he had forgotten her name. "How long was it?"

They always took too much time. He had to hurry them, force them to be economical.

At the end, like school, there was the final test. They seemed to do it all perfectly, the gestures, the cadences he had devised. He was timing them like runners. Two hours and twenty minutes.

"Marvelous," he told them.

That night Lang was drunk at the party the producer gave. It was in a small restaurant. The entry was filled with odors and displays of food, the cooks nodded from the kitchen. Fifty people were there, a hundred, crowded together and speaking different languages. Among them Anna shone like a queen. On her wrist was a new bracelet from Bulgari's, she had coolly demanded a discount, the clerk hadn't known what to say. She was in a slim gold suit that showed her breasts. Her strange, flat face seemed to float without expression among the others, sometimes she wore a faint, a drifting smile.

Lang felt depressed. He did not understand what they had been doing, the exaggerations dismayed him, he didn't believe in Iles, his energies, his insight, he didn't believe in any of it. He tried to calm himself. He saw them at the biggest table, the producer at Anna's elbow. They were talking, why was she so animated? They always come alive when the lights are on, someone said.

He watched Guivi. He could see Anna leaning across to him, her long hair, her throat.

"It's stupid to be making it in color," Lang said to the man beside him.

"What?" He was a film company executive. He had a face like a fish, a bass, that had gone bad. "What do you mean, not in color?"

"Black and white," Lang told him.

"What are you talking about? You can't sell a black and white film. Life is in color."

"Life?"

"Color is real," the man said. He was from New York. The ten greatest films of all time, the twenty greatest, were in color, he said.

"What about . . ." Lang tried to concentrate, his elbow slipped, "*The Bicycle Thief*?"

"I'm talking about modern films."

II.

Today was sunny. He was writing in brief, disconsolate phrases. *Yesterday it rained, it was dark until late afternoon, the day before was the same.* The corridors of the Inghilterra were vaulted like a convent, the doors set deep in the walls. Still, he thought, it was comfortable. He gave his shirts to the maid in the morning, they were back the next day. She did them at home. He had seen her bending over to take linen from a cabinet. The tops of her stockings showed—it was classic Buñuel—the mysterious white of a leg.

The girl from publicity called. They needed information for his biography.

"What information?"

"We'll send a car for you," she said.

It never came. He went the next day by taxi and waited thirty minutes in her office, she was in seeing the producer. Finally she returned, a thin girl with damp spots under the arms of her dress.

"You called me?" Lang said.

She did not know who he was.

"You were going to send a car for me."

"Mr. Lang," she suddenly cried. "Oh, I'm sorry."

The desk was covered with photos, the chairs with newspapers and magazines. She was an assistant, she had worked on *Cleopatra*, *The Bible*, *The Longest Day*. There was money to be earned in American films.

"They've put me in this little room," she apologized.

Her name was Eva. She lived at home. Her family ate without speaking, four of them in the sadness of bourgeois surroundings, the radio which didn't work, thin rugs on the floor. When he was finished, her father cleared his throat. The meat was better the last time, he said. The *last* time? her mother asked.

"Yes, it was better," he said.

"The last time it was tasteless."

"Ah, well, two times ago," he said.

They fell into silence again. There was only the sound of forks, an occasional glass. Suddenly her brother rose from the table and left the room. No one looked up.

He was crazy, this brother, well, perhaps not crazy but

enough to make them weep. He would remain for days in his room, the door locked. He was a writer. There was one difficulty, everything worthwhile had already been written. He had gone through a period when he devoured books, three and four a day, and could quote vast sections of them afterward, but the fever had passed. He lay on his bed now and looked at the ceiling.

Eva was nervous, people said. Of course she was nervous. She was thirty. She had black hair, small teeth, and a life in which she had already given up hope. They had nothing for his biography, she told Lang. They had to have a biography for everybody. She suggested finally he write it himself. Yes, of course, he imagined it would be something like that.

Her closest friend—like all Italians she was alert to friends and enemies—her most useful friend was an hysterical woman named Mirella Ricci who had a large apartment and aristocratic longings, also the fears and illnesses of women who live alone. Mirella's friends were homosexuals and women who were separated. She had dinner with them in the evening, she telephoned them several times a day. She was a woman with large nostrils and white skin, pale as paper, but she was still able to see white spots on it. Her doctor said they were a circulatory condition.

She was working on the film, like Eva. They talked of everyone, Iles: he knew actors, Mirella said. Whichever ones were brought in, he chose the best, well, he had made one or two mistakes. They were eating at Otello's, tortoises crawled on the floor. The script was interesting, Mirella said, but she didn't like the writer, he was cold. He was also a *frocio*, she knew the signs. As for the producer . . . she made a disgusted sound. He dyed his hair, she said. He looked thirty-nine but he was really fifty. He had already tried to seduce her.

"When?" Eva said.

They knew everything. They were like nurses whose tenderness was dead. It was they who ran the sickhouse. They knew how much money everyone was getting, who was not to be trusted.

The producer: first of all he was impotent, Mirella said. When he wasn't impotent, he was unwilling, the rest of the time he didn't know how to go about it and when he did, it was unsatisfactory. On top of that, he was a man who was always without a girl.

Her nostrils had darkness in them. She expected waiters to treat her well.

"How is your brother?" she said.

"Oh, the same."

"He still isn't working?"

"He has a job in a record shop but he won't be there long. They'll fire him."

"What is wrong with men?" she said.

"I'm exhausted," Eva sighed. She was haggard from late hours. She had to type letters for the producer because one of his secretaries was sick.

"He tried to make love to me, too," she admitted.

"Tell me," Mirella said.

"At his hotel . . ."

Mirella waited.

"I brought him some letters. He insisted I stay and talk. He wanted to give me a drink. Finally he tried to kiss me. He fell on his knees—I was cowering on the divan—and said, Eva, you smell so sweet. I tried to pretend it was all a joke."

The joys of rectitude. They drove around in little Fiats. They paid attention to their clothes.

The film was going well, a day ahead of schedule. Iles was working with a kind of vast assurance. He roamed around the great, black Mitchell in tennis shoes, he ate no lunch. The rushes were said to be extraordinary. Guivi never went to see them. Anna asked Lang about them, what did he think? He tried to decide. She was beautiful in them, he told her —it was true—there was a quality in her face which illumin-ated the entire film . . . he never finished. As usual, she was disinterested. She had already turned to someone else, the cameraman.

"Did you see them?" she said.

Iles wore an old sweater, the hair hung in his face. Two films a year, he repeated . . . that was the keystone of all his belief. Eisenstein only made six altogether, but he didn't work under the American system. Anyway, Iles had no confidence when he was at rest.

Whatever his weaknesses, his act of grandeur was in con-cealing the knowledge that the film was already wreckage: Guivi was simply not good enough, he worked without think-ing, he worked as one eats a meal. Iles knew actors.

Farewell, Guivi. It was the announcement of death. He was already beginning to enter the past. He signed auto-graphs, the space showing between his teeth. He charmed journalists. The perfect victim, he suspected nothing. The glory of his life had blinded him. He dined at the best tables, a bottle of fine Bordeaux before him. He mimicked the foolishness of Iles.

"Guivi, my love," he imitated, "the trouble is you are Russian, you are moody and violent. He's telling me what it is to be Russian. Next he'll start describing life under communism."

Anna was eating with very slow bites.

"Do you know something?" she said calmly.

He waited.

"I've never been so happy."

"Really?"

"Not in my whole life," she said.

He smiled. His smile was opera.

"With you I am the woman everyone believes I am," she said.

He looked at her long and deeply. His eyes were dark, the pupils invisible. Love scenes during the day, he thought wearily, love scenes at night. People were watching them from all around the room. When they rose to go, the waiters crowded near the door.

Within three years his career would be over. He would see himself in the flickering television as if it were some curious dream. He invested in apartment houses, he owned land in Spain. He would become like a woman, jealous, unforgiving, and perhaps one day in a restaurant even see Iles with a young actor, explaining with the heat of a fanatic some very ordinary idea. Guivi was thirty-seven. He had a moment on the screen that would never be forgotten. Tinted posters of him would peel from the sides of buildings more and more remote, the resemblance fading, his name becoming stale.

He would smile across alleys, into the sour darkness. Far-off dogs were barking. The streets smelled of the poor.

III.

There was a party for Anna's birthday at a restaurant in the outskirts, the restaurant in which Farouk, falling backward from the table, had died. Not everyone was invited. It was meant to be a surprise.

She arrived with Guivi. She was not a woman, she was a minor deity, she was some beautiful animal innocent of its grace. It was February, the night was cold. The chauffeurs waited inside the cars. Later they gathered quietly in the cloakroom.

"My love," Iles said to her, "you are going to be very, very happy."

"Really?"

He put his arm around her without replying; he nodded. The shooting was almost over. The rushes, he said, were the best he had ever seen. Ever.

"As for this fellow . . ." he said, reaching for Guivi.

The producer joined them.

"I want you for my next picture, both of you," he announced. He was wearing a suit a size too small, a velvet suit bought on Via Borgognona.

"Where did you get it?" Guivi said. "It's fantastic. Who is supposed to be the star here anyway?"

Posener looked down at himself. He smiled like a guilty boy.

"Do you like it?" he said. "Really?"

"No, where did you get it?"

"I'll send you one tomorrow."

"No, no . . ."

"Guivi, please," he begged, "I want to."

He was filled with goodwill, the worst was past. The actors had not run away or refused to work, he was overcome with love for them, as for a bad child who unexpectedly does something good. He felt he must do something in return.

"Waiter!" he cried. He looked around, his gestures always seemed wasted, vanished in empty air.

"Waiter," he called, "champagne!"

There were twenty or so people in the room, other actors, the American wife of a count. At the table Guivi told stories. He drank like a Georgian prince, he had plans for Geneva, Gstaad. There was the Italian producer, he said, who had an actress under contract, she was a second Sophia Loren. He had made a fortune with her. Her films were only shown in Italy, but everyone went to them, the money was pouring in. He always kept the journalists away, however, he never let them talk to her alone.

"Sellerio," someone guessed.

"Yes," said Guivi, "that's right. Do you know the rest of the story?"

"He sold her."

But half the contract only, Guivi said. Her popularity was fading, he wanted to get everything he could. There was a big ceremony, they invited all the press. She was going to sign. She picked up the pen and leaned forward a little for the photographers, you know, she had these enormous, eh . . .

well, anyway, on the paper she wrote: with his finger Guivi made a large X. The newsmen all looked at each other. Then Sellerio took the pen and very grandly, just below her name: Guivi made one X and next to it, carefully, another. Illiterate. That's the truth. They asked him, look, what is the second X for? You know what he told them? *Dottore.*

They laughed. He told them about shooting in Naples with a producer so cheap he threw a cable across the trolley wires to steal power. He was clever, Guivi, he was a storyteller in the tradition of the east, he could speak three languages. Later, when she finally understood what had happened, Anna remembered how happy he seemed this night.

"Shall we go on to the Hostaria?" the producer said.

"What?" Guivi asked.

"The Hostaria . . ." As with the waiters, it seemed no one heard him. "The Blue Bar. Come on, we're going to the Blue Bar," he announced.

Outside the Botanical Gardens, parked in the cold, the small windows of the car frosted, Lang sat. His clothing was open. His flesh was pale in the refracted light. He had eaten dinner with Eva. She had talked for hours in a low, uncertain voice, it was a night for stories, she had told him everything, about Coleman the head of publicity, Mirella, her brother, Sicily, life. On the road to the mountains which overlooked Palermo there were cars parked at five in the afternoon. In each one was a couple, the man with a handkerchief spread in his lap.

"I am so lonely," she said suddenly.

She had only three friends, she saw them all the time.

They went to the theater together, the ballet. One was an actress. One was married. She was silent, she seemed to wait. The cold was everywhere, it covered the glass. Her breath was in crystals, visible in the dark.

"Can I kiss it?" she said.

She began to moan then, as if it were holy. She touched it with her forehead. She was murmuring. The nape of her neck was bare.

She called the next morning. It was eight o'clock.

"I want to read something to you," she said.

He was half-asleep, the racket was already drifting up from the street. The room was chill and unlighted. Within it, distant as an old record, her voice was playing. It entered his body, it commanded his blood.

"I found this," she said. "Are you there?"

"Yes."

"I thought you would like it."

It was from an article. She began to read.

In February of 1868, in Milan, Prince Umberto had given a splendid ball. *In a room which blazed with light the young bride who was one day to be Queen of Italy was introduced. It was the event of the year, crowded and gay, and while the world of fashion amused itself thus, at the same hour and in the same city a lone astronomer was discovering a new planet, the ninety-seventh on Chacornac's chart. . . .*

Silence. A *new planet*.

In his mind, still warmed by the pillow, it seemed a sacred calm had descended. He lay like a saint. He was naked, his ankles, his hipbones, his throat.

He heard her call his name. He said nothing. He lay there

becoming small, smaller, vanishing. The room became a window, a facade, a group of buildings, squares and sections, in the end all of Rome. His ecstasy was beyond knowing. The roofs of the great cathedrals shone in the winter air.

LOST SONS

All afternoon the cars, many with out-of-state plates, were coming along the road. The long row of lofty brick quarters appeared above. The grey walls began.

In the reception area a welcoming party was going on. There were faces that had hardly changed at all and others like Reemstma's whose name tag was read more than once. Someone with a camera and flash attachment was running around in a cadet bathrobe. Over in the barracks they were drinking. Doors were open. Voices spilled out.

"Hooknose will be here," Dunning promised loudly. There was a bottle on the desk near his feet. "He'll show, don't worry. I had a letter from him."

"A letter? Klingbeil never wrote a letter."

"His secretary wrote it," Dunning said. He looked like a judge, large and well fed. His glasses lent a dainty touch. "He's teaching her to write."

"Where's he living now?"

"Florida."

"Remember the time we were sneaking back to Buckner at two in the morning and all of a sudden a car came down the road?"

Dunning was trying to arrange a serious expression.

95

"We dove in the bushes. It turned out it was a taxi. It slammed on the brakes and backed up. The door opens and there's Klingbeil in the backseat, drunk as a lord. Get in, boys, he says."

Dunning roared. His blouse with its rows of colored ribbons was unbuttoned, gluteal power hinted by the width of his lap.

"Remember," he said, "when we threw Devereaux's Spanish book with all his notes in it out the window? Into the snow. He never found it. He went bananas. You bastards, I'll kill you!"

"He'd have been a star man if he hadn't been living with you."

"We tried to broaden him," Dunning explained.

They used to do the sinking of the *Bismarck* while he was studying. Klingbeil was the captain. They would jump up on the desks. *Der Schiff ist kaputt!* they shouted. They were firing the guns. The rudder was jammed, they were turning in circles. Devereaux sat head down with his hands pressed over his ears. Will you bastards shut up! he screamed.

Bush, Buford, Jap Andrus, Doane, and George Hilmo were sitting on the beds and windowsill. An uncertain face looked in the doorway.

"Who's that?"

It was Reemstma whom no one had seen for years. His hair had turned grey. He smiled awkwardly. "What's going on?"

They looked at him.

"Come in and have a drink," someone finally said.

He found himself next to Hilmo, who reached across to

shake hands with an iron grip. "How are you?" he said. The others went on talking. "You look great."

"You, too."

Hilmo seemed not to hear. "Where are you living?" he said.

"Rosemont. Rosemont, New Jersey. It's where my wife's family's from," Reemstma said. He spoke with a strange intensity. He had always been odd. Everyone wondered how he had ever made it through. He did all right in class but the image that lasted was of someone bewildered by close order drill which he seemed to master only after two years and then with the stiffness of a cat trying to swim. He had full lips which were the source of an unflattering nickname. He was also known as To The Rear March because of the disasters he caused at the command.

He was handed a used paper cup. "Whose bottle is this?" he asked.

"I don't know," Hilmo said. "Here."

"Are a lot of people coming?"

"Boy, you're full of questions," Hilmo said.

Reemstma fell silent. For half an hour they told stories. He sat by the window, sometimes looking in his cup. Outside, the clock with its black numerals began to brighten. West Point lay majestic in the early evening, its dignified foliage still. Below, the river was silent, mysterious islands floating in the dusk. Near the corner of the library a military policeman, his arm moving with precision, directed traffic past a sign for the reunion of 1960, a class on which Vietnam had fallen as stars fell on 1915 and 1931. In the distance was the faint sound of a train.

It was almost time for dinner. There were still occasional cries of greeting from below, people talking, voices. Feet were leisurely descending the stairs.

"Hey," someone said unexpectedly, "what the hell is that thing you're wearing?"

Reemstma looked down. It was a necktie of red, flowered cloth. His wife had made it. He changed it before going out.

"Hello, there."

Walking calmly alone was a white-haired figure with an armband that read 1930.

"What class are you?"

"Nineteen-sixty," Reemstma said.

"I was just thinking as I walked along, I was wondering what finally happened to everybody. It's hard to believe but when I was here we had men who simply packed up after a few weeks and went home without a word to anyone. Ever hear of anything like that? Nineteen-sixty, you say?"

"Yes, sir."

"You ever hear of Frank Kissner? I was his chief of staff. He was a tough guy. Regimental commander in Italy. One day Mark Clark drove up and said, Frank, come here a minute, I want to talk to you. Haven't got time, I'm too busy, Frank said."

"Really?"

"Mark Clark said, Frank, I want to make you a B.G. I've got time, Frank said."

The mess hall, in which the alumni dinner was being held, loomed before them, its doors open. Its scale had always been heroic. It seemed to have doubled in size and was filled with the white of tablecloths as far as one could see.

The bars were crowded, there were lines fifteen and twenty deep of men waiting patiently. Many of the women were in dinner dresses. Above it all was the echoing haze of conversation.

There were those with the definite look of success, like Hilmo who wore a grey summer suit with a metallic sheen and to whom everyone liked to talk although he was given to abrupt silences, and there were also the unfading heroes, those who had been cadet officers, come to life again. Early form had not always held. Among those now of high rank were men who in their schooldays had been relatively undistinguished. Reemstma, who had been out of touch, was somewhat surprised by this. For him the hierarchy had never been altered.

A terrifying face blotched with red suddenly appeared. It was Cramner, who had lived down the hall.

"Hey, Eddie, how's it going?"

He was holding two drinks. He had just retired a year ago, Cramner said. He was working for a law firm in Reading.

"Are you a lawyer?"

"I run the office," Cramner said. "You married? Is your wife here?"

"No."

"Why not?"

"She couldn't come," Reemstma said.

His wife had met him when he was thirty. Why would she want to go, she had asked? In a way he was glad she hadn't. She knew no one and given the chance she would often turn the conversation to religion. There would be two weird people instead of one. Of course, he did not really think of himself as weird, it was only in their eyes. Perhaps not even. He was being greeted, talked to. The women, especially, unaware of established judgments, were friendly. He found himself talking to the lively wife of a classmate he vaguely remembered, R. C. Walker, a lean man with a somewhat sardonic smile.

"You're a what?" she said in astonishment. "A painter? You mean an artist?" She had thick, naturally curly blonde hair and a pleasant softness to her cheeks. Her chin had a slight double fold. "I think that's fabulous!" She called to a friend, "Nita, you have to meet someone. It's Ed, isn't it?"

"Ed Reemstma."

"He's a painter," Kit Walker said exuberantly.

Reemstma was dazed by the attention. When they learned that he actually sold things they were even more interested.

"Do you make a living at it?"

"Well, I have a waiting list for paintings."

"You do!"

He began to describe the color and light—he painted landscapes—of the countryside near the Delaware, the shape of the earth, its furrows, hedges, how things changed slightly from year to year, little things, how hard it was to do the sky. He described the beautiful, glinting green of a hummingbird his wife had brought to him. She had found it in the garage; it was dead, of course.

"Dead?" Nita said.

"The eyes were closed. Except for that, you wouldn't have known."

He had an almost wistful smile. Nita nodded warily.

Later there was dancing. Reemstma would have liked to

go on talking but people drifted away. Tables broke up after dinner into groups of friends.

"Bye for now," Kit Walker said.

He saw her talking to Hilmo, who gave him a brief wave. He wandered about for a while. They were playing "Army Blue." A wave of sadness went through him, memories of parades, the end of dances, Christmas leave. Four years of it, the classes ahead leaving in pride and excitement, unknown faces filling in behind. It was finished, but no one turns his back on it completely. The life he might have led came back to him, almost whole.

Outside barracks, late at night, five or six figures were sitting on the steps, drinking and talking. Reemstma sat near them, not speaking, not wanting to break the spell. He was one of them again, as he had been on frantic evenings when they cleaned rifles and polished their shoes to a mirrorlike gleam. The haze of June lay over the great expanse that separated him from those endless tasks of years before. How deeply he had immersed himself in them. How ardently he had believed in the image of a soldier. He had known it as a faith, he had clung to it dumbly, as a cripple clings to God.

In the morning Hilmo trotted down the stairs, tennis shorts tight over his muscled legs, and disappeared through one of the sally ports for an early match. His insouciance was unchanged. They said that before the Penn State game when he had been first string the coach had pumped them up telling them they were not only going to beat Penn State, they were going to beat them by two touchdowns, then turning to Hilmo, "And who's going to be the greatest back in the East?"

"I don't know. Who?" Hilmo said.

Empty morning. As usual, except for sports there was little to do. Shortly after ten they formed up to march to a memorial ceremony at the corner of the Plain. Before a statue of Sylvanus Thayer they stood at attention, one tall maverick head in a cowboy hat, while the choir sang "The Corps." The thrilling voices, the solemn, staggered parts rose through the air. Behind Reemstma someone said quietly, "You know, the best friends I ever had or ever will have are the ones I had here."

Afterward they walked out to take their places on the parade ground. The superintendent, a trim lieutenant general, stood not far off with his staff and the oldest living graduate, who was in a wheelchair.

"Look at him," Dunning said. He was referring to the superintendent. "That's what's wrong with this place. That's what's wrong with the whole army."

Faint waves of band music beat toward them. It was warm. There were bees in the grass. The first miniature formations of cadets, bayonets glinting, began to move into view. Above, against the sky, a lone distinguished building, and that a replica, stood. The chapel. Many Sundays with their manly sermons on virtue and the glittering choir marching toward the door with graceful, halting tread, gold stripes shining on the sleeves of the leaders. Down below, partly hidden, the gymnasium, the ominous dark patina on everything within, the floor, the walls, the heavy boxing gloves. There were champions enshrined there who would never be unseated, maxims that would never be erased.

At the picnic it was announced that of the 550 original members, 529 were living and 176 present so far.

"Not counting Klingbeil!"

"Okay, one seventy-six plus a possible Klingbeil."

"An *im*possible Klingbeil," someone called out.

There was a brief cheer.

The tables were in a large, screened pavilion on the edge of the lake. Reemstma looked for Kit Walker. He'd caught sight of her earlier, in the food line, but now he could not find her. She seemed to have gone. The class president was speaking.

"We got a card from Joe Waltsak. Joe retired this year. He wanted to come but his daughter's graduating from high school. I don't know if you know this story. Joe lives in Palo Alto and there was a bill before the California legislature to change the name of any street an All-American lived on and name it after him. Joe lives on Parkwood Drive. They were going to call it Waltsak Drive, but the bill didn't pass, so instead they're calling him Joe Parkwood."

The elections were next. The class treasurer and the vice-president were not running again. There would have to be nominations for these.

"Let's have somebody different for a change," someone commented in a low voice.

"Somebody we know," Dunning said.

"You want to run, Mike?"

"Yeah, sure, that would be great," Dunning muttered.

"How about Reemstma?" It was Cramner, the blossoms of alcoholism ablaze in his face. The edges of his teeth were uneven as he smiled, as if eaten away.

"Good idea."

"Who, me?" Reemstma said. He was flustered. He looked around in surprise.

"How about it, Eddie?"

He could not tell if they were serious. It was all off-handed—the way Grant had been picked from obscurity one evening when he was sitting on a bench in St. Louis. He murmured something in protest. His face had become red.

Other names were being proposed. Reemstma felt his heart pounding. He had stopped saying, no, no, and sat there, mouth open a bit in bewilderment. He dared not look around him. He shook his head slightly, no. A hand went up, "I move that the nominations be closed."

Reemstma felt foolish. They had tricked him again. He felt as if he had been betrayed. No one was paying any attention to him. They were counting raised hands.

"Come on, you can't vote," someone said to his wife.

"I can't?" she said.

Wandering around as the afternoon ended Reemstma finally caught sight of Kit Walker. She acted a little strange. She didn't seem to recognize him at first. There was a grass stain on the back of her white skirt.

"Oh, hello," she said.

"I was looking for you."

"Would you do me a favor?" she said. "Would you mind getting me a drink? My husband seems to be ignoring me."

Though Reemstma did not see it, someone else was ignoring her, too. It was Hilmo, standing some way off. They had taken care to come back to the pavilion separately. Friends who would soon be parting were talking in small groups, their faces shadowy against the water that glistened behind them. Reemstma returned with some wine in a plastic glass.

"Here you are. Is anything wrong?"

"Thank you. No, why? You know, you're very nice," she said. She had noticed something over his shoulder. "Oh, dear."

"What?"

"Nothing. It looks like we're going."

"Do you have to?" he managed to say.

"Rick's over by the door. You know him, he hates to be kept waiting."

"I was hoping we could talk."

He turned. Walker was standing outside in the sunlight. He was wearing an aloha shirt and tan slacks. He seemed somewhat aloof. Reemstma was envious of him.

"We have to drive back to Belvoir tonight," she said.

"I guess it's a long way."

"It was very nice meeting you," she said.

She left the drink untouched on the corner of the table. Reemstma watched her make her way across the floor. She was not like the others, he thought. He saw them walking to their car. Did she have children? he found himself wondering. Did she really find him interesting?

In the hour before twilight, at six in the evening, he heard the noise and looked out. Crossing the area toward them was the unconquerable schoolboy, long-legged as a crane, the ex-infantry officer now with a small, well-rounded paunch, waving both arms.

Dunning was bellowing from a window, "Hooknose!"

"Look who I've got!" Klingbeil called back.

He was with Devereaux, the tormented scholar. Their arms were around each other's shoulders. They were crossing together, grinning, friends since cadet days, friends for life. They started up the stairs.

"Hooknose!" Dunning shouted.

Klingbeil threw open his arms in mocking joy.

He was the son of an army officer. As a boy he had sailed on the Matson Line and gone back and forth across the country. He told stories of seduction in the lower berth. My son, my son, she was moaning. He was irredeemable, he had the common touch, his men adored him. Promoted slowly, he had gotten out and become a land developer. He drove a green Cadillac famous in Tampa. He was a king of poker games, drinking, late nights.

She had probably not meant it, Reemstma was thinking. His experience had taught him that. He was not susceptible to lies.

"Oh," wives would say, "of course. I think I've heard my husband talk about you."

"I don't know your husband," Reemstma would say.

A moment of alarm.

"Of course, you do. Aren't you in the same class?"

He could hear them downstairs.

"*Der Schiff ist kaputt!*" they were shouting. "*Der Schiff ist kaputt!*"

AKHNILO

It was late August. In the harbor the boats lay still, not the slightest stirring of their masts, not the softest clink of a sheave. The restaurants had long since closed. An occasional car, headlights glaring, came over the bridge from North Haven or turned down Main Street, past the lighted telephone booths with their smashed receivers. On the highway the discotheques were emptying. It was after three.

In the darkness Fenn awakened. He thought he had heard something, a slight sound, like the creak of a spring, the one on the screen door in the kitchen. He lay there in the heat. His wife was sleeping quietly. He waited. The house was unlocked though there had been many robberies and worse nearer the city. He heard a faint thump. He did not move. Several minutes passed. Without making a sound he got up and went carefully to the narrow doorway where some stairs descended to the kitchen. He stood there. Silence. Another thump and a moan. It was Birdman falling to a different place on the floor.

Outside, the trees were like black reflections. The stars were hidden. The only galaxies were the insect voices that filled the night. He stared from the open window. He was still not sure if he had heard anything. The leaves of the immense beech that overhung the rear porch were close enough to touch. For what seemed a long time he examined the shadowy area around the trunk. The stillness of everything made him feel visible but also strangely receptive. His eyes drifted from one thing to another behind the house, the pale Corinthian columns of the arbor next door, the mysterious hedge, the garage with its rotting sills. Nothing.

Eddie Fenn was a carpenter though he'd gone to Dartmouth and majored in history. Most of the time he worked alone. He was thirty-four. He had thinning hair and a shy smile. Not much to say. There was something quenched in him. When he was younger it was believed to be some sort of talent, but he had never really set out in life, he had stayed close to shore. His wife, who was tall and nearsighted, was from Connecticut. Her father had been a banker. *Of Greenwich and Havana* the announcement in the papers had said—he'd managed the branch of a New York bank there when she was a child. That was in the days when Havana was a legend and millionaires committed suicide after smoking a last cigar.

Years had passed. Fenn gazed out at the night. It seemed he was the only listener to an infinite sea of cries. Its vastness awed him. He thought of all that lay concealed behind it, the desperate acts, the desires, the fatal surprises. That afternoon he had seen a robin picking at something near the edge of the grass, seizing it, throwing it in the air, seizing it again: a toad, its small, stunned legs fanned out. The bird threw it again. In ravenous burrows the blind shrews hunted ceaselessly, the pointed tongues of reptiles were testing the air, there was the crunch of abdomens, the passivity of the trapped, the soft throes of mating. His daughters were asleep down the hall. Nothing is safe except for an hour.

As he stood there the sound seemed to change, he did not know how. It seemed to separate as if permitting something to come forth from it, something glittering and remote. He tried to identify what he was hearing as gradually the cricket, cicada, no, it was something else, something feverish and strange, became more clear. The more intently he listened, the more elusive it was. He was afraid to move for fear of losing it. He heard the soft call of an owl. The darkness of the trees which was absolute seemed to loosen, and through it that single, shrill note.

Unseen the night had opened. The sky was revealing itself, the stars shining faintly. The town was sleeping, abandoned sidewalks, silent lawns. Far off among some pines was the gable of a barn. It was coming from there. He still could not identify it. He needed to be closer, to go downstairs and out the door, but that way he might lose it, it might become silent, aware.

He had a disturbing thought, he was unable to dislodge it: it *was* aware. Quivering there, repeating and repeating itself above the rest, it seemed to be coming only to him. The rhythm was not constant. It hurried, hesitated, went on. It was less and less an instinctive cry and more a kind of signal, a code, not anything he had heard before, not a collection of long and short impulses but something more intricate, in a way almost like speech. The idea frightened him. The words, if that was what they were, were piercing and thin but the awareness of them made him tremble as if they were the combination to a vault.

Beneath the window lay the roof of the porch. It sloped gently. He stood there, perfectly still, as if lost in thought. His heart was rattling. The roof seemed wide as a street. He would have to go out on it hoping he was unseen, moving silently, without abruptness, pausing to see if there was a change in the sound to which he was now acutely sensitive. The darkness would not protect him. He would be entering a night of countless networks, shifting eyes. He was not sure if he should do it, if he dared. A drop of sweat broke free and ran quickly down his bare side. Tirelessly the call continued. His hands were trembling.

Unfastening the screen, he lowered it carefully and leaned it against the house. He was moving quietly, like a serpent, across the faded green roofing. He looked down. The ground seemed distant. He would have to hang from the roof and drop, light as a spider. The peak of the barn was still visible. He was moving toward the lodestar, he could feel it. It was almost as if he were falling. The act was dizzying, irreversible. It was taking him where nothing he possessed would protect him, taking him barefoot, alone.

As he dropped to the ground, Fenn felt a thrill go through him. He was going to be redeemed. His life had not turned out as he expected but he still thought of himself as special, as belonging to no one. In fact he thought of failure as romantic. It had almost been his goal. He carved birds, or he had. The tools and partially shaped blocks of wood were on a table in the basement. He had, at one time, almost become a naturalist. Something in him, his silence, his willingness to be apart, was adapted to that. Instead he began to build furniture with a friend who had some money, but the business failed. He was drinking. One morning he woke up lying by the car in the worn ruts of the driveway, the old woman who lived across the street warning away her dog. He went inside before his children saw him. He was very close, the doctor told him frankly, to being an alcoholic. The words astonished him. That was long ago. His family had saved him, but not without cost.

He paused. The earth was firm and dry. He went toward the hedge and across the neighbor's driveway. The tone that was transfixing him was clearer. Following it he passed behind houses he hardly recognized from the back, through neglected yards where cans and rubbish were hidden in dark grass, past empty sheds he had never seen. The ground began to slope gently down, he was nearing the barn. He could hear the voice, *his* voice, pouring overhead. It was coming from somewhere in the ghostly wooden triangle rising like the face of a distant mountain brought unexpectedly close by a turn of the road. He moved toward it slowly, with the fear of an explorer. Above him he could hear the thin stream trilling. Terrified by its closeness he stood still.

At first, he later remembered, it meant nothing, it was too glistening, too pure. It kept pouring out, more and more insane. He could not identify, he could never repeat, he could not even describe the sound. It had enlarged, it was pushing everything else aside. He stopped trying to comprehend it and instead allowed it to run through him, to invade him like a chant. Slowly, like a pattern that changes its appearance as one stares at it and begins to shift into another dimension, inexplicably the sound altered and exposed its real core. He began to recognize it. It *was* words. They had no meaning, no antecedents, but they were unmistakably a language, the first ever heard from an order vaster and more dense than our own. Above, in the whitish surface, desperate, calling, was the nameless pioneer.

In a kind of ecstasy he moved closer. Instantly he realized it was wrong. The sound hesitated. He closed his eyes in anguish but too late, it faltered and then stopped. He felt stupid, shamed. He stepped back a little, helplessly. All about him the voices clattered. The night was filled with them. He turned this way and that hoping to find it, but the thing he had heard was gone.

It was late. The first pale cast had come to the sky. He was standing near the barn with the fragments of a dream one must struggle to remember: four words, distinct and inimitable, that he had made out. Protecting them, concentrating on them with all his strength, he began to carry them back. The cries of the insects seemed louder. He was afraid something would happen, a dog would bark, a light go on in a bedroom and he would be distracted, he would lose his hold. He had to get back without seeing anything, without hearing anything, without thinking. He was repeating the words to himself as he went, his lips moving steadily. He hardly dared breathe. He could see the house. It had turned grey. The windows were dark. He had to get to it. The sound of the night creatures seemed to swell in torment and rage, but he was beyond that. He was escaping. He had gone an immense distance, he was coming to the hedge. The porch was not far away. He stood on the railing, the eave of the roof within reach. The rain gutter was firm, he pulled himself up. The crumbling green asphalt was warm beneath his feet. One leg over the sill, then the other. He was safe. He stepped back from the window instinctively. He had done it. Outside, the light seemed faint and historic. A spectral dawn began to come through the trees.

Suddenly he heard the floor creak. Someone was there, a figure in the soft light drained of color. It was his wife, he was stunned by the image of her holding a cotton robe about her, her face made plain by sleep. He made a gesture as if to warn her off.

"What is it? What's wrong?" she whispered.

He backed away making vague movements with his hands. His head was sideways, like a horse. He was moving backward. One eye was on her.

"What is it?" she said, alarmed. "What happened?"

No, he pleaded, shaking his head. A word had dropped away. No, no. It was fluttering apart like something in the sea. He was reaching blindly for it.

Her arm went around him. He pulled away abruptly. He closed his eyes.

"Darling, what is it?" He was troubled, she knew. He had never really gotten over his difficulty. He often woke at night, she would find him sitting in the kitchen, his face looking tired and old. "Come to bed," she invited.

His eyes were closed tightly. His hands were over his ears.

"Are you all right?" she said.

Beneath her devotion it was dissolving, the words were spilling away. He began to turn around frantically.

"What is it, what is it?" she cried.

The light was coming everywhere, pouring across the lawn. The sacred whispers were vanishing. He could not spare a moment. Hands clapped to his head he ran into the hall searching for a pencil while she ran after, begging him to tell her what was wrong. They were fading, there was just one left, worthless without the others and yet of infinite value. As he scribbled the table shook. A picture quivered on the wall. His wife, her hair held back with one hand, was peering at what he had written. Her face was close to it.

"What is that?"

Dena, in her nightgown, had appeared in a doorway awakened by the noise.

"What is it?" she asked.

"Help me," her mother cried.

"Daddy, what happened?"

Their hands were reaching for him. In the glass of the picture a brilliant square of blue and green was trembling, the luminous foliage of the trees. The countless voices were receding, turning into silence.

"What is it, what is it?" his wife pleaded.

"Daddy, please!"

He shook his head. He was nearly weeping as he tried to pull away. Suddenly he slumped to the floor and sat there and for Dena they had begun again the phase she remembered from the years she was first in school when unhappiness filled the house and slamming doors and her father clumsy with affection came into their room at night to tell them stories and fell asleep at the foot of her bed.

DUSK

Mrs. Chandler stood alone near the window in a tailored suit, almost in front of the neon sign that said in small red letters PRIME MEATS. She seemed to be looking at onions, she had one in her hand. There was no one else in the store. Vera Pini sat by the cash register in her white smock, staring at the passing cars. Outside it was cloudy and the wind was blowing. Traffic was going by in an almost continuous flow. "We have some good Brie today," Vera remarked without moving. "We just got it in."

"Is it really good?"

"Very good."

"All right, I'll take some." Mrs. Chandler was a steady customer. She didn't go to the supermarket at the edge of town. She was one of the best customers. Had been. She didn't buy that much anymore.

On the plate glass the first drops of rain appeared. "Look at that. It's started," Vera said.

Mrs. Chandler turned her head. She watched the cars go by. It seemed as if it were years ago. For some reason she found herself thinking of the many times she had driven out herself or taken the train, coming into the country, stepping down onto the long, bare platform in the darkness, her husband or a child there to meet her. It was warm. The trees were huge and black. Hello, darling. Hello, Mummy, was it a nice trip?

The small neon sign was very bright in the greyness, there was the cemetery across the street and her own car, a foreign one, kept very clean, parked near the door, facing in the wrong direction. She always did that. She was a woman who lived a certain life. She knew how to give dinner parties, take care of dogs, enter restaurants. She had her way of answering invitations, of dressing, of being herself. Incomparable habits, you might call them. She was a woman who had read books, played golf, gone to weddings, whose legs were good, who had weathered storms, a fine woman whom no one now wanted.

The door opened and one of the farmers came in. He was wearing rubber boots. "Hi, Vera," he said.

She glanced at him. "Why aren't you out shooting?"

"Too wet," he said. He was old and didn't waste words. "The water's a foot high in a lot of places."

"My husband's out."

"Wish you'd told me sooner," the old man said slyly. He had a face that had almost been obliterated by the weather. It had faded like an old stamp.

It was shooting weather, rainy and blurred. The season had started. All day there had been the infrequent sound of guns and about noon a flight of six geese, in disorder, passed over the house. She had been sitting in the kitchen and heard their foolish, loud cries. She saw them through the window. They were very low, just above the trees.

The house was amid fields. From the upstairs, distant barns and fences could be seen. It was a beautiful house, for years she had felt it was unique. The garden was tended, the wood stacked, the screens in good repair. It was the same inside, everything well selected, the soft white sofas, the rugs and chairs, the Swedish glasses that were so pleasant to hold, the lamps. The house is my soul, she used to say.

She remembered the morning the goose was on the lawn, a big one with his long black neck and white chinstrap, standing there not fifteen feet away. She had hurried to the stairs. "Brookie," she whispered.

"What?"

"Come down here. Be quiet."

They went to the window and then on to another, looking out breathlessly.

"What's he doing so near the house?"

"I don't know."

"He's big, isn't he?"

"Very."

"But not as big as Dancer."

"Dancer can't fly."

All gone now, pony, goose, boy. She remembered that night they came home from dinner at the Werners' where there had been a young woman, very pure featured, who had abandoned her marriage to study architecture. Rob Chandler had said nothing, he had merely listened, distracted, as if to a familiar kind of news. At midnight in the kitchen, hardly having closed the door, he simply announced it. He had turned away from her and was facing the table.

"What?" she said.

He started to repeat it but she interrupted.

"What are you saying?" she said numbly.

He had met someone else.

"You've what?"

She kept the house. She went just one last time to the apartment on Eighty-second Street with its large windows from which, cheek pressed to glass, you could see the entrance steps of the Met. A year later he remarried. For a while she veered off course. She sat at night in the empty living room, almost helpless, not bothering to eat, not bothering to do anything, stroking her dog's head and talking to him, curled on the couch at two in the morning still in her clothes. A fatal weariness had set in, but then she pulled herself together, began going to church and putting on lipstick again.

Now as she returned to her house from the market, there were great, leaden clouds marbled with light, moving above the trees. The wind was gusting. There was a car in the driveway as she turned in. For just a moment she was alarmed and then she recognized it. A figure came toward her.

"Hi, Bill," she said.

"I'll give you a hand." He took the biggest bag of groceries from the car and followed her into the kitchen.

"Just put it down on the table," she said. "That's it. Thanks. How've you been?"

He was wearing a white shirt and a sport coat, expensive at one time. The kitchen seemed cold. Far off was the faint pop of guns.

"Come in," she said. "It's chilly out here."

"I just came by to see if you had anything that needed to be taken care of before the cold weather set in."

"Oh, I see. Well," she said, "there's the upstairs bathroom. Is that going to be trouble again?"

"The pipes?"

"They're not going to break again this year?"

"Didn't we stuff some insulation in there?" he said. There was a slight, elegant slur in his speech, back along the edge of his tongue. He had always had it. "It's on the north side, is the trouble."

"Yes," she said. She was searching vaguely for a cigarette. "Why do you suppose they put it there?"

"Well, that's where it's always been," he said.

He was forty but looked younger. There was something hard and hopeless about him, something that was preserving his youth. All summer on the golf course, sometimes into December. Even there he seemed indifferent, dark hair blowing—even among companions, as if he were killing time. There were a lot of stories about him. He was a fallen idol. His father had a real-estate agency in a cottage on the highway. Lots, farms, acreage. They were an old family in these parts. There was a lane named after them.

"There's a bad faucet. Do you want to take a look at that?"

"What's wrong with it?"

"It drips," she said. "I'll show you."

She led the way upstairs. "There," she said, pointing toward the bathroom. "You can hear it."

He casually turned the water on and off a few times and felt under the tap. He was doing it at arm's length with a slight, careless movement of the wrist. She could see him from the bedroom. He seemed to be examining other things on the counter.

She turned on a light and sat down. It was nearly dusk and the room immediately became cozy. The walls were papered in a blue pattern and the rug was a soft white. The polished stone of the hearth gave a sense of order. Outside, the fields were disappearing. It was a serene hour, one she shrank from. Sometimes, looking toward the ocean, she thought of her son, although that had happened in the sound and long ago. She no longer found she returned to it every day. They said it got better after a time but that it never really went away. As with so many other things, they were right. He had been the youngest and very spirited though a little frail. She prayed for him every Sunday in church. She prayed just a simple thing: O Lord, don't overlook him, he's very small. . . . Only a little boy, she would sometimes add. The sight of anything dead, a bird scattered in the road, the stiff legs of a rabbit, even a dead snake, upset her.

"I think it's a washer," he said. "I'll try and bring one over sometime."

"Good," she said. "Will it be another month?"

"You know Marian and I are back together again. Did you know that?"

"Oh, I see." She gave a slight, involuntary sigh. She felt strange. "I, uh . . ." What weakness, she thought later. "When did it happen?"

"A few weeks ago."

After a bit she stood up. "Shall we go downstairs?"

She could see their reflections passing the stairway window. She could see her apricot-colored shirt go by. The wind was still blowing. A bare branch was scraping the side of the house. She often heard that at night.

"Do you have time for a drink?" she asked.

"I'd better not."

She poured some Scotch and went into the kitchen to get some ice from the refrigerator and add a little water. "I suppose I won't see you for a while."

It hadn't been that much. Some dinners at the Lanai, some improbable nights. It was just the feeling of being with someone you liked, someone easy and incongruous. "I . . ." She tried to find something to say.

"You wish it hadn't happened."

"Something like that."

He nodded. He was standing there. His face had become a little pale, the pale of winter.

"And you?" she said.

"Oh, hell." She had never heard him complain. Only about certain people. "I'm just a caretaker. She's my wife. What are you going to do, come up to her sometime and tell her everything?"

"I wouldn't do that."

"I hope not," he said.

When the door closed she did not turn. She heard the car start outside and saw the reflection of the headlights. She stood in front of the mirror and looked at her face coldly. Forty-six. It was there in her neck and beneath her eyes. She would never be any younger. She should have pleaded, she thought. She should have told him all she was feeling, all that suddenly choked her heart. The summer with its hope and long days was gone. She had the urge to follow him, to drive past his house. The lights would be on. She would see someone through the windows.

That night she heard the branches tapping against the house and the window frames rattle. She sat alone and thought of the geese, she could hear them out there. It had gotten cold. The wind was blowing their feathers. They lived a long time, ten or fifteen years, they said. The one they had seen on the lawn might still be alive, settled back into the fields with the others, in from the ocean where they went to be safe, the survivors of bloody ambushes. Somewhere in the wet grass, she imagined, lay one of them, dark sodden breast, graceful neck still extended, great wings striving to beat, bloody sounds coming from the holes in its beak. She went around and turned on lights. The rain was coming down, the sea was crashing, a comrade lay dead in the whirling darkness.

VIA NEGATIVA

There is a kind of minor writer who is found in a room of the library signing his novel. His index finger is the color of tea, his smile filled with bad teeth. He knows literature, however. His sad bones are made of it. He knows what was written and where writers died. His opinions are cold but accurate. They are pure, at least there is that.

He's unknown, though not without a few admirers. They are really like marriage, uninteresting, but what else is there? His life is his journals. In them somewhere is a line from the astrologer: your natural companions are women. Occasionally, perhaps. No more than that. His hair is thin. His clothes are a little out of style. He is aware, however, that there is a great, a final glory which falls on certain figures barely noticed in their time, touches them in obscurity and recreates their lives. His heroes are Musil and, of course, Gerard Manley Hopkins. Bunin.

There are writers like P in an expensive suit and fine English shoes who come walking down the street in eye-splintering sunlight, the crowd seeming to part for them, to leave an opening like the eye of a storm.

"I hear you got a fortune for your book."

"What? Don't believe it," they say, though everyone knows. On close examination, the shoes are even handmade.

Their owner has a rich head of hair. His face is powerful, his brow, his long nose. A suffering face, strong as a door. He recognizes his questioner as someone who has published several stories. He only has a moment to talk.

"Money doesn't mean anything," he says. "Look at me. I can't even get a decent haircut."

He's serious. He doesn't smile. When he came back from London and was asked to endorse a novel by a young acquaintance he said, let him do it the way I did, on his own. They all want something, he said.

And there are old writers who owe their eminence to the *New Yorker* and travel in wealthy circles like W, who was famous at twenty. Some critics now feel his work is shallow and too derivative—he had been a friend of the greatest writer of our time, a writer who inspired countless imitators, perhaps it would be better to say one of the great writers, not everyone is in agreement, and I don't want to get into arguments. They broke up later anyway, W didn't like to say why.

His first, much-published story—everyone knows it—brought him at least fifty women over the years, he used to say. His wife was aware of it. In the end he broke with her, too. He was not a man who kept his looks. Small veins began to appear in his cheeks. His eyes became red. He insulted people, even waiters in restaurants. Still, in his youth he was said to have been very generous, very brave. He was against injustice. He gave money to the Loyalists in Spain.

Morning. The dentists are laying out their picks. In the doorways, as the sun hits them, the bums begin to groan. Nile went on the bus to visit his mother, the words of Victor Hugo about *all the armies in the world being unable to stop an idea whose time has come* on an advertisement above his head. His hair was uncombed. His face had the arrogance, the bruised lips of someone determined to live without money. His mother met him at the door and took this pale face in her hands. She stepped back to see better. She was trembling slightly with a steady, rhythmic movement.

"Your teeth," she said.

He covered them with his tongue. His aunt came from the kitchen to embrace him.

"Where have you been?" she cried. "Guess what we're having for lunch."

Like many fat women, she liked to laugh. She was twice a widow, but one drink was enough to make her dance. She went to set the table. Passing the window, she glanced out. There was a movie house across the street.

"Degenerates," she said.

Nile sat between them, pulling his chair close to the table with little scrapes. They had not bothered to dress. The warmth of family lunches when the only interest is food. He was always hungry when he came. He ate a slice of bread heavy with butter as he talked. There was scrod and sautéed onions on a huge dish. Voices everywhere—the television was going, the radio in the kitchen. His mouth was full as he answered their questions.

"It's a little flat," his mother announced. "Did you cook it the same way?"

"Exactly the same," his aunt said. She tasted it herself. "It may need salt."

"You don't put salt on seafood," his mother said.

Nile kept eating. The fish fell apart beneath his fork, moist and white, he could taste the faint iodine of the sea. He knew the very market where it had been displayed on ice, the Jewish owner who did not shave. His aunt was watching him.

"Do you know something?" she said.

"What?"

She was not speaking to him. She had made a discovery.

"For a minute then, while he was eating, he looked just like his father."

A sudden, sweet pause opened in the room, a depth that had not been there when they were talking only of immorality and the danger of the blacks. His mother looked at him reverently.

"Did you hear that?" she asked. Her voice was hushed, she longed for the myths of the past. Her eyes had darkness around them, her flesh was old.

"How do you look like him?" She wanted to hear it recited.

"I don't," he said.

They did not hear him. They were arguing about his childhood, various details of it, poems he had memorized, his beautiful hair. What a good student he had been. How grownup when he ate, the fork too large for his hand. His chin was like his father's, they said. The shape of his head.

"In the back," his aunt said.

"A beautiful head," his mother confirmed. "You have a perfect head, did you know that?"

Afterward he lay on the couch and listened as they cleared the dishes. He closed his eyes. Everything was familiar to him, phrases he had heard before, quarrels about the past, even the smell of the cushions beneath his head. In the bedroom was a collection of photographs in ill-fitting frames. In them, if one traced the progression, was a face growing older and older, more and more unpromising. Had he really written all those earnest letters preserved in shoe boxes together with schoolbooks and folded programs? He was sleeping in the museum of his life.

He left at four. The doorman was reading the newspaper, his collar unbuttoned, the air surrounding him rich with odors of cooking. He didn't bother to look up as Nile went out. He was absorbed in a description of two young women whose bound bodies had been found on the bank of a canal. There were no pictures, only those from a high-school year-book. It was June. The street was lined with cars, the gutters melting.

The shops were closed. In their windows, abandoned to afternoon, were displays of books, cosmetics, leather clothes. He lingered before them. A great longing for money, a thirst rose in him, a desire to be recognized. He was walking for the hundredth time on streets which in no way acknowledged him, past endless apartments, consulates, banks. He came to the fifties, behind the great hotels. The streets were dank, like servants' quarters. Paper lay everywhere, envelopes, empty packages of cigarettes.

In Jeanine's apartment it was better. The floor was polished. Her breath seemed sweet.

"Have you been out?" he asked her.

"No, not yet."

"The streets are melting," he said. "You weren't working, were you?"

"I was reading."

From her windows one could see the second-floor salon in the rear of the Plaza in which hairdressers worked. It was red, with mirrors that multiplied its secrets. Naked, on certain afternoons, they had watched its silent acts.

"What are you reading?" he asked.

"Gogol."

"Gogol . . ." He closed his eyes and began to recite, "*In the carriage sat a gentleman, not handsome but not bad-looking, not too stout and not too thin, not old, but not so very young . . .*"

"What a memory you have."

"Listen, what novel is this? *For a long time I used to go to bed early . . .*"

"That's too easy," she said.

She was sitting on the couch, her legs drawn up beneath her, the book near her hand.

"I guess it is," he said. "Did you know this about Gogol? He died a virgin."

"Is that true?"

"The Russians are a little curious that way," he said. "Chekhov himself thought once a year was sufficient for a writer."

He had told her that before, he realized.

"Not everyone agrees with that," he murmured. "You know who I saw on the street yesterday? Dressed like a banker. Even his shoes."

"Who?"

Nile described him. After a moment she knew who he must be talking about.

"He's written a new book," she said.

"So I hear. I thought he was going to hold out his ring for me to kiss. I said, listen, tell me one thing, honestly: all the money, the attention . . ."

"You didn't."

Nile smiled. The teeth his mother wept over were revealed.

"He was terrified. He knew what I was going to say. He had everything, everybody was talking about him, and all I had was a pin. A needle. If I pushed, it would go straight to the heart."

She had a boy's face and arms with a faint shadow of muscle. Her fingernails were bitten clean. The afternoon light which had somehow found its way into the room gleamed from her knees. She was from Montana. When they first met, Nile had seen her as complaisant, which excited him, even stupid, but he discovered it was only a vast distance, perhaps of childhood, which surrounded her. She revealed herself in simple, unexpected acts, like a farmboy undressing. As she sat on the couch, one arm was exposed beside her. Within its elbow he could see the long, rich artery curved down to her wrist. It was full. It lay without beating.

She had been married. Her past astonished him. Her body bore no trace of it, not even a memory, it seemed. All she had learned was how to live alone. In the bathroom were soaps with the name printed on them, soaps that had never been wet. There were fresh towels, flowers in a blue glass. The bed was flat and smooth. There were books, fruit, announcements stuck in the edge of the mirror.

"What did you actually ask him?" she said.

"Do you have any wine?" Nile said. While she was gone,

he continued in a louder voice, "He's afraid of me. He's afraid of me because I've accomplished nothing."

He looked up. Plaster was flaking from the ceiling.

"You know what Cocteau said," he called. "There's a fame worse than failure. I asked him if he thought he really deserved it all."

"And what did he say?"

"I don't remember. What's this?" He took the bottle of sea-colored glass she carried. The label was slightly stained. "A Pauillac. I don't remember this. Did I buy it?"

"No."

"I didn't think so." He smelled it. "Very good. Someone gave it to you," he suggested.

She filled his glass.

"Do you want to go to a film?" he asked.

"I don't think so."

He looked at the wine.

"No?" he said.

She was silent. After a moment she said, "I can't."

He began to inspect titles in the bookcase near him, many he had never read.

"How's your mother?" he asked. "I like your mother." He opened one of the books. "Do you write to her?"

"Sometimes."

"You know, Viking is interested in me," he said abruptly. "They're interested in my stories. They want me to expand *Lovenights*."

"I've always liked that story," she said.

"I'm already working. I'm getting up very early. They want me to have a photograph made."

"Who did you see at Viking?"

"I forget his name. He's, uh . . . dark hair, he's about my size. I should know his name. Well, what's the difference?"

She went into the bedroom to change her clothes. He started to follow her.

"Don't," she said.

He sat down again. He could hear occasional, ordinary sounds, drawers opening and being shut, periods of silence. It was as if she were packing.

"Where are you going?" he called, looking at the floor.

She was brushing her hair. He could hear the swift, rhythmic strokes. She was facing herself in the mirror, not even aware of him. He was like a letter lying on the table, the half-read Gogol, like the wine. When she emerged, he could not look at her. He sat slouched, like a passionate child.

"Jeanine," he said, "I know I've disappointed you. But it's true about Viking."

"I know."

"I'll be very busy. . . . Do you have to go just now?"

"I'm a bit late."

"No, you're not," he said. "Please."

She could not answer.

"Anyway, I have to go home and work," he said. "Where are you going?"

"I'll be back by eleven," she said. "Why don't you call me?" She tried to touch his hair.

"There's more wine," she said. She no longer believed in him. In things he might say, yes, but not in him. She had lost her faith.

"Jeanine . . ."

"Good-bye, Nile," she said. It was the way she ended telephone calls.

She was going to the nineties, to dinner in an apartment she had not seen. Her arms were bare. Her face seemed very young.

When the door closed, panic seized him. He was suddenly desperate. His thoughts seemed to fly away, to scatter like birds. It was a deathlike hour. On television, the journalists were answering complex questions. The streets were still. He began to go through her things. First the closets. The drawers. He found her letters. He sat down to read them, letters from her brother, her lawyer, people he did not know. He began pulling forth everything, shirts, underclothes, long clinging weeds which were stockings. He kicked her shoes away, spilled open boxes. He broke her necklaces, pieces rained to the floor. The wildness, the release of a murderer filled him. As she sat there in the nineties, sometimes speaking a little, the men nearby uncertain, seeking to hold her glance, he whipped her like a yelping dog from room to room, pushing her into walls, tearing her clothes. She was stumbling, crying, he felt the horror of his acts. He had no right to them—why did this justify everything?

He was bathed in sweat, breathless, afraid to stay. He closed the door softly. There were old newspapers piled in the hall, the faint sounds from other apartments, children returning from errands to the store.

In the street he saw on every side, in darkening windows, in reflections, as if suddenly it were visible to him, a kind of chaos. It welcomed, it acclaimed him. The huge tires of buses roared past. It was the last hour of light. He felt the solitude of crime. He stopped, like an addict, in a phone booth. His legs were weak. No, beneath the weakness was something else. For a moment he saw unknown depths to himself, he glittered with images. It seemed he was attracting the glances of women who passed. They recognize me, he thought, they smell me in the dark like mares. He smiled at them with the cracked lips of an incorrigible. He cared nothing for them, only for the power to disturb. He was bending their love toward him, a stupid love, a love without which he could not breathe.

It was late when he arrived home. He closed the door. Darkness. He turned on the light. He had no sense of belonging there. He looked at himself in the bathroom mirror. There was a skylight over his head, the panes were black. He sat beneath the small, nude photograph of a girl he had once lived with, the edges were curled, and began to play, the G was sticking, the piano was out of tune. In Bach there was not only order and coherence but more, a code, a repetition which everything depended on. After a while he felt a pounding beneath his feet, the broom of the idiot on the floor below. He continued to play. The pounding grew louder. If he had a car . . . Suddenly the idea broke over him as if it were the one thing he had been trying to think of: a car. He would be speeding from the city to find himself at dawn on long, country roads. Vermont, no, further, Newfoundland, where the coast was still deserted. That was it, a car, he saw it plainly. He saw it parked in the gentle light of daybreak, its body stained from the journey, a faintly battered body that had survived some terrible, early crash.

All is chance or nothing is chance. That evening Jeanine

met a man who longed, he said, to perform an act of great and unending generosity, like Genet's in giving his house to a former lover.

"Did he do that?" she asked.

"They say."

It was P. The room was filled with people, and he was speaking to her, quite naturally, as if they had met before. She did not wonder what to say to him, she did not have to say anything. He was quite near. The fine wrinkles in his brow were visible, wrinkles not yet deepened.

"Generosity purifies," he said. He was later to tell her that words were no accident, their arrangement and choice was like another voice speaking, a voice which revealed everything. Vocabulary was like fingerprints, he said, like handwriting, like the body which revealed the invisible soul, which expressed it.

His face was dark, his features deep. He was part of another, a mysterious race. She was aware of how different her own face was with its wide mouth, its grey eyes, slow, curious, clear as a stream. She was aware also that the dress she wore, the depth of the chairs, the dimensions of this room afloat now in evening, all of these were part of an immersion into the flow of a great life. Her heart was beating slowly but hard. She had never felt so sure of herself, so bewildered by the ease with which it all was opening.

"I'm suspicious and grasping," he said. He was beginning his confessions. "I recognize that." Later he told her that in his entire life he had only been free for an hour, and that hour was always with her.

She asked no questions. She recognized him. In her own

apartment the lights were burning. The air of the city, bitter as acid, was absolutely still. She did not breathe it. She was breathing another air. She had not smiled once as yet. He later told her that this was the most powerful thing of all that had attracted him. Her breasts, he said, were like those of black tribal girls in the *National Geographic*.

THE DESTRUCTION OF THE
GOETHEANUM

In the garden, standing alone, he found the young woman who was a friend of the writer William Hedges, then unknown but even Kafka had lived in obscurity, she said, and so moreover had Mendel, perhaps she meant Mendeleyev. They were staying in a little hotel across the Rhine. No one could seem to find it, she said.

The river there flowed swiftly, the surface was alive. It carried things away, broken wood and branches. They spun around, went under, emerged. Sometimes pieces of furniture passed, ladders, windows. Once, in the rain, a chair.

They were living in the same room, but it was completely platonic. Her hand, he noticed, bore no ring or jewelry of any kind. Her wrists were bare.

"He doesn't like to be alone," she said. "He's struggling with his work." It was a novel, still far from finished though parts were extraordinary. A fragment had been published in Rome. "It's called *The Goetheanum*," she said. "Do you know what that is?"

He tried to remember the curious word already dissolving in his mind. The lights inside the house had begun to appear in the blue evening.

"It's the one great act of his life."

The hotel she had spoken of was small with small rooms and letters in yellow across the facade. There were many buildings like it. From the cool flank of the cathedral it was visible amid them, below and a little downstream. Also through the windows of antique shops and alleys.

Two days later he saw her from a distance. She was unmistakable. She moved with a kind of negligent grace, like a dancer whose career is ended. The crowd ignored her.

"Oh," she greeted him, "yes, hello."

Her voice seemed vague. He was sure she did not recognize him. He didn't know exactly what to say.

"I was thinking about some of the things you told me . . ." he began.

She stood with people pushing past, her arms filled with packages. The street was hot. She did not understand who he was, he was certain of it. She was performing simple errands, those of a remote and saintly couple.

"Forgive me," she said, "I'm really not myself."

"We met at Sarren's," he explained.

"Yes, I know."

A silence followed. He wanted to say something quite simple to her but she was preventing it.

She had been to the museum. When Hedges worked he had to be alone, sometimes she would find him asleep on the floor.

"He's crazy," she said. "Now he's sure there'll be a war. Everything's going to be destroyed."

Her own words seemed to disinterest her. The crowd was pulling her away.

"Can I walk with you for a minute?" he asked. "Are you going toward the bridge?"

She looked both ways.

"Yes," she decided.

They went down the narrow streets. She said nothing. She glanced in shop windows. She had a mouth which curved downward, a serving girl's mouth, a girl from small towns.

"Are you interested in painting?" he heard her say.

"Yes."

In the museum there were Holbeins and Hodlers, El Grecos, Max Ernst. The silence of long salons. In them one understood what it meant to be great.

"Do you want to go tomorrow?" she said. "No, tomorrow we're going somewhere. Perhaps the day after?"

That day he woke early, already nervous. The room seemed empty. The sky was yellow with light. The surface of the river, between stone banks, was incandescent. The water rushed in fragments white as fire, at their center one could not even look.

By nine the sky had faded, the river was broken into silver. At ten it was brown, the color of soup. Barges and old-fashioned steamers were working slowly upstream or going swiftly down. The piers of the bridges trailed small wakes.

A river is the soul of a city, only water and air can purify. At Basel, the Rhine lies between well-established stone banks. The trees are carefully trimmed, the old houses hidden behind them.

He looked for her everywhere. He crossed the Rhein-brucke and, watching faces, went to the open market through the crowds. He searched among the stalls. Women were buying flowers, they boarded streetcars and sat with the bunches in their laps. In the Borse restaurant fat men were eating, their small ears close to their heads.

She was nowhere to be found. He even entered the cathedral, expecting for a moment to find her waiting. There was no one. The city was turning to stone. The pure hour of sunlight had passed, there was nothing left now but a raging afternoon that burned his feet. The clocks struck three. He gave up and returned to the hotel. There was an edge of white paper in his box. It was a note, she would meet him at four.

In excitement he lay down to think. She had not forgotten. He read it again. Were they really meeting in secret? He was not certain what that meant. Hedges was forty, he had almost no friends, his wife was somewhere back in Connecticut, he had left her, he had renounced the past. If he was not great, he was following the path of greatness which is the same as disaster, and he had the power to make one devote oneself to his life. She was with him constantly. I'm never out of his sight, she complained. Nadine: it was a name she had chosen herself.

She was late. They ended up going to tea at five o'clock; Hedges was busy reading English newspapers. They sat at a table overlooking the river, the menus in their hands long and slim as airline tickets. She seemed very calm. He wanted to keep looking at her. *Hummersalat*, he was reading somehow, *rump steak*. She was very hungry, she announced. She had been at the museum, the paintings made her ravenous.

"Where were you?" she said.

Suddenly he realized she had expected him. There were young couples strolling the galleries, their legs washed in sunlight. She had wandered among them. She knew quite well what they were doing: they were preparing for love. His eyes slipped.

"I'm starving," she said.

She ate asparagus, then a goulash soup, and after that a cake she did not finish. The thought crossed his mind that perhaps they had no money, she and Hedges, that it was her only meal of the day.

"No," she said. "William has a sister who's married to a very rich man. He can get money there."

It seemed she had the faintest accent. Was it English?

"I was born in Genoa," she told him.

She quoted a few lines of Valéry which he later found out were incorrect. *Afternoons torn by wind, the stinging sea . . .* She adored Valéry. An anti-Semite, she said.

She described a trip to Dornach, it was forty minutes away by streetcar, then a long walk from the station where she had stood arguing with Hedges about which way to go, it always annoyed her that he had no sense of direction. It was uphill, he was soon out of breath.

Dornach had been chosen by the teacher Rudolf Steiner to be the center of his realm. There, not far from Basel, beyond the calm suburbs, he had dreamed of establishing a community with a great central building to be named after Goethe, whose ideas had inspired it, and in 1913 the corner-stone for it was finally laid. The design was Steiner's own, as were all the details, techniques, the paintings, the specially engraved glass. He invented its construction just as he had its shape.

It was to be built entirely of wood, two enormous domes

which intersected, the plot of that curve itself was a mathematical event. Steiner believed only in curves, there were no right angles anywhere. Small, tributary domes like helmets contained the windows and doors. Everything was wood, everything except the gleaming Norwegian slates that covered the roof. The earliest photographs showed it surrounded by scaffolding like some huge monument, in the foreground were groves of apple trees. The construction was carried on by people from all over the world, many of them abandoned professions and careers. By the spring of 1914 the roof timbers were in position, and while they were still laboring the war broke out. From the nearby provinces of France they could actually hear the rumble of cannon. It was the hottest month of summer.

She showed him a photograph of a vast, brooding structure.

"The Goetheanum," she said.

He was silent. The darkness of the picture, the resonance of the domes began to invade him. He submitted to it as to the mirror of a hypnotist. He could feel himself slipping from reality. He did not struggle. He longed to kiss the fingers which held the postcard, the lean arms, the skin which smelled like lemons. He felt himself trembling, he knew she could see it. They sat like that, her gaze was calm. He was entering the grey, the Wagnerian scene before him which she might close at any moment like a matchbox and replace in her bag. The windows resembled an old hotel somewhere in middle Europe. In Prague. The shapes sang to him. It was a fortification, a terminal, an observatory from which one could look into the soul.

"Who is Rudolf Steiner?" he asked.

He hardly heard her explanation. He was beginning to have ecstasies. Steiner was a great teacher, a savant who believed deep insights could be revealed in art. He believed in movements and mystery plays, rhythms, creation, the stars. Of course. And somehow from this she had learned a scenario. She had become the illusionist of Hedges' life.

It was Hedges, the convict Joyce scholar, the rumpled ghost at literary parties, who had found her. He was distant at first, he barely spoke a word to her the night they met. She had not been in New York long then. She was living on Twelfth Street in a room with no furniture. The next day the phone rang. It was Hedges. He asked her to lunch. He had known from the first exactly who she was, he said. He was calling from a phone booth, the traffic was roaring past.

"Can you meet me at Haroot's?" he said.

His hair was uncombed, his fingers unsteady. He was sitting by the wall, too nervous to look at anything except his hands. She became his companion.

They spent long days together wandering in the city. He wore shirts the color of blue ink, he bought her clothes. He was wildly generous, he seemed to care nothing for money, it was crumpled in his pockets like wastepaper, when he paid for things it would fall on the floor. He made her come to restaurants where he was dining with his wife and sit at the bar so he could watch her while they ate.

Slowly he began her introduction to another world, a world which scorned exposure, a world more rich than the one she knew, certain occult books, philosophies, even music. She discovered she had a talent for it, an instinct. She achieved a kind of power over herself. There were periods of deep affection, serenity. They sat in a friend's house and listened to Scriabin. They ate at the Russian Tea Room, the waiters knew his name. Hedges was performing an extraordinary act, he was fusing her life. He, too, had found a new existence: he was a criminal at last. At the end of a year they came to Europe.

"He's intelligent," she explained. "You feel it immediately. He has a mind that touches everything."

"How long have you been with him?"

"Forever," she said.

They walked back toward her hotel in that one, dying hour which ends the day. The trees by the river were black as stone. *Wozzeck* was playing at the theater to be followed by *The Magic Flute*. In the print shops were maps of the city and drawings of the famous bridge as it looked in Napoleon's time. The banks were filled with newly minted coins. She was strangely silent. They stopped once, before a restaurant with a tank of fish, great speckled trout larger than a shoe lazing in green water, their mouths working slowly. Her face was visible in the glass like a woman's on a train, indifferent, alone. Her beauty was directed toward no one. She seemed not to see him, she was lost in her thoughts. Then, coldly, without a word, her eyes met his. They did not waver. In that moment he realized she was worth everything.

They had not had an easy time. Reason is unequal to man's problems, Hedges said. His wife had somehow gotten hold of his bank account, not that it was much, but she had a nose like a ferret, she found other earnings that might have come his way. Further, he was sure his letters to his children were not being delivered. He had to write them at school and in care of friends.

The question above all and always, however, was money. It was crushing them. He wrote articles but they were hard to sell, he was no good at anything topical. He did a piece about Giacometti with many haunting quotations which were entirely invented. He tried everything. Meanwhile, on every side it seemed, young men were writing film scripts or selling things for enormous sums.

Hedges was alone. The men his age had made their reputations, everything was passing him by. Anyway he often felt it. He knew the lives of Cervantes, Stendhal, Italo Svevo but none of them was as improbable as his own. And wherever they went there were his notebooks and papers to carry. Nothing is heavier than paper.

In Grasse he had trouble with his teeth, something went bad in the roots of old repairs. He was in misery, they had to pay a French dentist almost every penny they had. In Venice he was bitten by a cat. A terrible infection developed, his arm swelled to twice its size, it seemed the skin would burst. The *cameriera* told them cats had venom in their mouth like snakes, the same thing had happened to her son. The bites were always deep, she said, the poison entered the blood. Hedges was in agony, he could not sleep. It would have been much worse fifty years ago, the doctor told them. He touched a point up near his shoulder. Hedges was too weak to ask what it meant. Twice a day a woman came with a hypodermic in a battered tin box and gave him shots. He was growing more feverish. He could no longer read. He wanted to dictate some final things, Nadine took them down. He insisted on being buried with her photograph over his heart, he had made her promise to tear it from her passport.

"How will I get home?" she had asked.

Beneath them in the sunlight the great river flowed, almost without a sound. The lives of artists seem beautiful at last, even the terrible arguments about money, the nights there is nothing to do. Besides, through it all, Hedges was never helpless. He lived one life and imagined ten others, he could always find refuge in one of them.

"But I'm tired of it," she confessed. "He's selfish. He's a child."

She did not look like a woman who had suffered. Her clothes were silky. Her teeth were white. On the far pathways couples were having lunch, the girls with their shoes off, their feet slanting down the bank. They were throwing bits of bread in the water.

The development of the individual had reached its apogee, Hedges believed, that was the essence of our time. A new direction must be found. He did not believe in collectivism, however. That was a blind road. He wasn't certain yet of what the path would be. His writing would reveal it, but he was working against time, against a tide of events, he was in exile, like Trotsky. Unfortunately, there was no one to kill him. It didn't matter, his teeth would do it in the end, he said.

Nadine was staring into the water.

"There are nothing but eels down there," she said.

He followed her gaze. The surface was impenetrable. He tried to find a single, black shadow betrayed by its grace.

"When the time comes to mate," she told him, "they go to the sea."

She watched the water. When the time came they heard somehow, they slithered across meadows in the morning, shining like dew. She was fourteen years old, she told him, when her mother took her favorite doll down to the river and threw it in, the days of being a young girl were over.

"What shall I throw in?" he asked.

She seemed not to hear. Then she looked up.

"Do you mean that?" she finally said.

She wanted them to have dinner together, would Hedges sense something or not? He tried not to think about it or allow himself to be alarmed. There were scenes in every literature of this moment, but still he could not imagine what it would be like. A great writer might say, I know I cannot keep her, but would he dare give her up? Hedges, his teeth filled with cavities and all the years lying on top of his unwritten works?

"I owe him so much," she had said.

Still, it was difficult to face the evening calmly. By five o'clock he was in a state of nerves, playing solitaire in his room, rereading articles in the paper. It seemed that he had forgotten how to speak about things, he was conscious of his facial expressions, nothing he did seemed natural. The person he had been had somehow vanished, it was impossible to create another. Everything was impossible, he imagined a dinner at which he would be humiliated, deceived.

At seven o'clock, afraid the telephone would ring at any moment, he went down in the elevator. The glimpse of himself in the mirror reassured him, he seemed ordinary, he seemed calm. He touched his hair. His heart was thundering. He looked at himself again. The door slid open. He stepped out, half expecting to find them there. There was no one. He turned the pages of the Zurich paper while keeping an eye on the door. Finally he managed to sit in one of the chairs. It was awkward. He moved. It was seven-ten. Twenty minutes later an old Citroën backed straight into the grill of a Mercedes parked in the street with a great smashing of glass. The concierge and desk clerk went running out. There were pieces everywhere. The driver of the Citroën was opening his door.

"Oh, Christ," he murmured, looking around.

It was William Hedges. Alone.

They all began to talk at once. The owner of the Mercedes, which was blinded, fortunately was not present. A policeman was making his way along the street.

"Well, it's not too serious," Hedges said. He was inspecting his own car. The taillights were shattered. There was a dent in the trunk.

After much discussion he was finally allowed to enter the hotel. He was wearing a striped cotton jacket and a shirt the color of ink. He had a white face, damp with sweat, the face of an unpopular schoolboy, high forehead, thinning hair, a soft beard touched with grey, the beard of an explorer, a man who washed his socks in the Amazon.

"Nadine will be along a little later," he said.

When he reached for a drink, his hand was trembling.

"My foot slipped off the brake," he explained. He quickly lit a cigarette. "The insurance pays that, don't they? Probably not."

He seemed to have reached a stop, the first of many enormous pauses during which he looked in his lap. Then, as if it were the thing he had been struggling to think of, he inquired painfully, "What do you . . . think of Basel?"

The headwaiter had placed them on opposite sides of the table, the empty chair between them. Its presence seemed to weigh on Hedges. He asked for another drink. Turning, he knocked over a glass. That act, somehow, relieved him. The waiter dabbed at the wet tablecloth with a napkin. Hedges spoke around him.

"I don't know exactly what Nadine has told you," he said softly. A long pause. "She sometimes tells . . . fantastic lies."

"Oh, yes?"

"She's from a little town in Pennsylvania," Hedges muttered. "Julesberg. She's never been . . . she was just a . . . an ordinary girl when we met."

They had come to Basel to visit certain institutions, he explained. It was an . . . interesting city. History has certain sites upon which whole epochs turn, and the village of Dornach gave evidence of a very . . . The sentence was never finished. Rudolf Steiner had been a student of Goethe. . . .

"Yes, I know."

"Of course. Nadine's been telling you, hasn't she?"

"No."

"I see."

He finally began again, about Goethe. The range of that intellect, he said, had been so extraordinary that he was able, like Leonardo before him, to encompass all of what was then human knowledge. That, in itself, implied an overall . . . coherence, and the fact that no man had been capable of it since could easily mean the coherence no longer existed, it was dissolved. . . . The ocean of things known had burst its shores.

"We are on the verge," Hedges said, "of radical departures in the destiny of man. Those who reveal them . . ."

The words, coming with agonized slowness, seemed to take forever. They were a ruse, a feint. It was difficult to hear them out.

". . . will be torn to pieces like Galileo."

"Is that what you think?"

A long pause again.

"Oh, yes."

They had another drink.

"We are a little strange, I suppose, Nadine and I," Hedges said, as if to himself.

It was finally the time.

"I don't think she's a very happy woman."

There was a moment of silence.

"Happy?" Hedges said. "No, she isn't happy. She isn't capable of being happy. Ecstasies. She is ecstatic. She tells me so every day," he said. He put his hand to his forehead, half covering his eyes. "You see, you don't know her at all."

She was not coming, suddenly that was clear. There was going to be no dinner.

Something should have been said, it ended too vaguely. Ten minutes after Hedges had gone, leaving behind an embarrassing expanse of white and three places set, the thought came of what he should have demanded: I want to talk to her.

All doors had closed. He was miserable, he could not imagine someone with weaknesses, incapacities like his own. He had intended to mutilate a man and it turned into monologue— probably they were laughing about it at that very moment. It had all been humiliating. The river was moving beneath his window, even in darkness the current showed. He stood looking down upon it. He walked about trying to calm himself. He lay on the bed, it seemed his limbs were trembling. He detested himself. Finally he was still.

He had just closed his eyes when in the emptiness of the room the telephone rang. It rang again. A third time. Of course! He had expected it. His heart was jumping as he picked it up. He tried to say hello quite calmly. A man's voice answered. It was Hedges. He was humble.

"Is Nadine there?" he managed to say.

"Nadine?"

"Please, may I speak to her," Hedges said.

"She's not here."

There was a silence. He could hear Hedges' helpless breathing. It seemed to go on and on.

"Look," Hedges began, his voice was less brave, "I just want to talk to her for a moment, that's all. . . . I beg you . . ."

She was somewhere in the town then, he hurried out to find her. He didn't bother to decide where she might be. Somehow the night had turned in his direction, everything was changing. He walked, he ran through the streets, afraid to be late.

It was nearly midnight, people were coming out of the theaters, the café at the Casino was roaring. A sea of hidden and half-hidden faces with the waiters always standing so someone could be hidden behind them, he combed it slowly. Surely she was there. She was sitting at a table by herself, she expected to be found.

The same cars were turning through the streets, he stepped among them. People walked slowly, stopping at lighted windows. She would be looking at a display of expensive shoes, antique jewelry perhaps, gold necklaces. At the corners he had a feeling of loss. He passed down interior arcades. He was leaving the more familiar section. The newsstands were locked, the cinemas dark.

Suddenly, like the first truth of illness, the certainty left him. Had she gone back to her hotel? Perhaps she was even at his, or had been there and gone. He knew she was capable of aimless, original acts. Instead of drifting in the darkness of the city, her somewhat languid footsteps existing only to be devoured by his, instead of choosing a place in which to be found as cleverly as she had drawn him to follow, she might have become discouraged and returned to Hedges to say only, I felt like a walk.

There is always one moment, he thought, it never comes again. He began going back, as if lost, along streets he had already seen. The excitement was gone, he was searching, he was no longer sure of his instincts but wondering instead what she might have decided to do.

On the stairway near the Heuwaage, he stopped. The

square was empty. He was suddenly cold. A lone man was passing below. It was Hedges. He was wearing no tie, the collar of his jacket was turned up. He walked without direction, he was in search of his dreams. His pockets had bank notes crumpled in them, cigarettes bent in half. The whiteness of his skin was visible from afar. His hair was uncombed. He did not pretend to be young, he was past that, into the heart of his life, his failed work, a man who took commuter trains, who drank tea, hoping for something, some proof in the end that his talents had been as great as the others'. This world is giving birth to another, he said. We are nearing the galaxy's core. He was writing that, he was inventing it. His poems would become our history.

The streets were deserted, the restaurants had turned out their lights. Alone in a café in the repetition of empty tables, the chairs placed upon them upside down, his dark shirt, his doctor's beard, Hedges sat. He would never find her. He was like a man out of work, an invalid, there was no place to go. The cities of Europe were silent. He coughed a little in the chill.

The Goetheanum of the photograph, the one she had shown him, did not exist. It had burned on the night of December 31, 1922. There had been an evening lecture, the audience had gone home. The night watchman discovered smoke and soon afterward the fire became visible. It spread with astonishing rapidity and the firemen battled without effect. At last the situation seemed beyond hope. An inferno was rising within the great windows. Steiner called everyone out of the building. Exactly at midnight the main dome was breached, the flames burst through and roared upward.

The windows with their special glass were glowing, they began to explode from the heat. A huge crowd had come from the nearby villages and even from Basel itself where, miles away, the fire was visible. Finally the dome collapsed, green and blue flames soaring from the metal organ pipes. The Goetheanum disappeared, its master, its priest, its lone creator walking slowly in the ashes at dawn.

A new structure made of concrete rose in its place. Of the old, only photos remained.

DIRT

Billy was under the house. It was cool there, it smelled of the unturned earth of fifty years. A kind of rancid dust sifted down through the floorboards and fell on his face like a light rain. He spit it out. He turned his head and, reaching carefully up, wiped around his eyes with the sleeve of his shirt. He looked back toward the strip of daylight at the edge of the house. Harry's legs were in the sun—every so often, with a groan, he would kneel down and see how it was going.

They were leveling the floor of the old Bryant place. Like all of them it had no foundation, it sat on pieces of wood.

"Feller could start right there," Harry called.

"This one?"

"That's it."

Billy slowly wiped the dirt from his eyes again and began to set up the jack. The joists were a few inches above his face.

They ate lunch sitting outside. It was hot, mountain weather. The sun was dry, the air thin as paper. Harry ate slowly. He had a wrinkled neck and white stubble along his jowl line.

Death was coming for Harry Mies. He would lie emptied, his cheeks rouged, the fine, old man's ears unhearing. There was no telling the things he knew. He was alone in the far fields of his life. The rain fell on him, he did not move.

There are animals that finally, when the time comes, will not lie down. He was like that. When he kneeled he would get up again slowly. He would rise to one knee, pause, and finally sway to his feet like an old horse.

"Feller in town with all the hair . . ." he said.

Billy's fingers made black marks on the bread.

"The hair?"

"What's he supposed to be?"

"I think a drummer," Billy said.

"A drummer."

"He's with a band."

"Must be with something," Harry said.

He unscrewed the cap from a battered thermos and poured what looked like tea. They sat in the quiet of the tall cottonwoods, not even the highest leaves were moving.

They drove to the dump, the sun in the windshield was burning their knees. There was an old cattle gate salvaged from somewhere, some bankrupt ranch. It was open, Harry drove in. They were in a field of junk and garbage on the edge of the creek, a bare field forever smoldering. A black man in overalls appeared from a shack surrounded by bedsprings. He was round-shouldered, heavy as a bull. There was an old green Chrysler parked on the far side.

"Looking for some pipe, Al," Harry said.

The man said nothing. He gave a sort of halfhearted signal. Harry had already gone past and turned down an alley of old furniture, stoves, aluminum chairs. There was a sour smell in the air. A few refrigerators, indestructible, had fallen down the bank and were lying half-buried in the stream.

The pipe was all in one place. It was mostly rusted, Billy kicked aimlessly at some sections.

"We can use it," Harry commented.

They began carrying pieces back to the car and put them on the roof. They drove slowly, the old man's head tilted back a little. The car swayed in and out of holes. The pipe rolled in the rack.

"Pretty good feller, Al," Harry said. They were coming to the shack. He lifted his hand as they passed. No one was there.

Billy's mind was wandering. The ride to town seemed long.

"They give him a lot of trouble," Harry said. He was watching the road, the empty road which connects all these towns.

"There's none of that stuff much good out there," he said. "Sometimes he tries to charge a little for it. People feel like they ought to be able to carry it off for nothing."

"He didn't charge you."

"Me? No, I bring him a little something now and then," Harry said. "Old Al and me are friends."

After a while, "Claims to be a free country, I dunno . . ." he said.

The cowboys at Gerhart's called him the Swede, but he never went in there. They would see him go by outside, papery skin, dangling arms, the slowness of age as he walked. He may have looked a little Swedish, pale-eyed from those mornings of invincible white, mornings of the great Southwest, black coffee in his cup, the day ahead. The ashtrays on the bar were plastic, the clock had the name of a whiskey printed on its face.

It was five-thirty. Billy walked in.

"There he is."

He ignored them.

"What'll it be, then?" Gerhart said.

"Beer."

On the wall was the stuffed head of a bear with a pair of glasses on its nose and a red plaster tongue. Above it hung an American flag with a sign: NO DOGS ALLOWED. Around the middle of the day there were a few people like Wayne Garrich who had the insurance agency, they wore straw rancher's hats rolled at the sides. Later there were construction workers in T-shirts and sunglasses, gas company men. It was always crowded after five. The ranch hands sat together at the tables with their legs stretched out. They had belt buckles with a gold-plated steerhead on them.

"Be thirty cents," Gerhart said. "What're you up to? Still working for old Harry?"

"Yeah, well . . ." Billy's voice wandered.

"What's he paying you?"

He was too embarrassed to tell the truth.

"Two fifty an hour," Billy said.

"Jesus Christ," Gerhart said. "I pay that for sweeping floors."

Billy nodded. He had no reply.

Harry took three dollars an hour himself. There were probably people in town would take more, he said, but that was his rate. He'd pour a foundation for that, he said, take three weeks.

There was not one day of rain. The sun laid on their backs like boards.

Harry got the shovel and hoe from the trunk of his car. He was tall, he carried them in one hand. He turned the wheelbarrow right side up, the bags of cement were piled beneath on a piece of plywood. He flushed out the wheelbarrow with the hose. Then he began mixing the first load of concrete: five shovels of gravel, three of sand, one of cement. Occasionally he'd stop and pick out a twig or piece of grass. The sun beat down like flats of tin. Ten thousand days of it down in Texas and all around. He turned the dry mixture over upon itself again and again, finally he began adding water. He added more water, working it in. The color became a rich, river-grey, the smooth face broken by gravel. Billy stood watching.

"Don't want it too runny," the old man said. There was always the feeling he might be talking to himself. He laid down the hoe. "Okey-dokey," he said.

His shoulders were stooped, they had the set of labor in them. He took the handles of the barrow without straightening up.

"I'll get it," Billy said, reaching.

"That's all right," Harry muttered. His teeth whistled on the "s."

He wheeled it himself, the surface now smooth and shifting a little from side to side, and set it down with a jolt near the wooden forms he'd built—Billy had dug the trench. Checking them one last time, he tilted the wheelbarrow and the heavy liquid fell from its lip. He scraped it empty and then moved along the trench with his shovel, jabbing to fill the voids. On the second trip he let Billy push the barrow, naked to the waist, the sun roaring down on his shoulders and back, his muscles jumping as he lifted. The next day he let him shovel.

Billy lived near the Catholic church, in a room on the ground floor. It had a metal shower. He slept without sheets, in the morning he drank milk from the carton. He was going out with a girl named Alma who was a waitress at Daly's. She had legs with hard calves. She didn't say much, her complaisance drove him crazy, sometimes she was at Gerhart's with someone else in a haze of voices, the bark of laughter, famous heavyweights behind her tacked on the wall. There were water stains near the ceiling. The door to the men's room slammed.

They talked about her. They stood at the bar so they could see her by turning a little. She was a girl in a small town. The television had exhibition football coming from Grand Junction. They were thinking of her legs as they watched the game, she was like an animal they wanted. She smoked a lot, Alma, but her teeth were white. She was flat-faced, like a fighter. She would be living in the trailer park, Billy told her. Her kids would eat white bread in big soft packages from the Woody Creek Store.

"Oh, yeah?"

She didn't deny it. She looked away. Like an animal, it didn't matter how pure they were, how beautiful. They went down the highway in clattering steel trucks, wisps of straw blowing clear as they passed. They were watched by the cold eyes of cowboys. They entered the house of blood, its sudden bone-cleaving blows, its muffled cries. He didn't spend much money on her—he was saving up. She never mentioned it.

They poured the side of the house that faced Third Street and started along the front. He thought of her in the sunlight that was browning his arms. He lifted the heavy barrow and became strong everywhere, like a tightened cable. When they finished in the evening, Harry washed off everything with the hose, he put the shovel and hoe in the trunk of his car. He sat on the front seat with the door open. He smiled to himself. He lifted his cap and smoothed his hair.

"Say," he said. There was something he wanted to tell. He looked at the ground. "Ever been West?"

It was a story of California in the thirties. There was a whole bunch of them going from town to town, looking for work. One day they came to a place, he forgot the name, and went into some little restaurant. You could get a whole meal for thirty cents in those days, but when they came to pay the check, the owner told them it would cost a dollar fifty each. If they didn't like it, he said, there was the state police just down the street. Afterward Harry walked over to the barbershop—he looked like that musician, he had so much hair. The barber put the sheet around him. Haircut, Harry told him. Then, hey, wait a minute, how much will it be? The barber had the scissors in his hand. I see you been eating over to the Greek's, he said.

He laughed a little, almost shyly. He glanced at Billy, his long teeth showed. They were his own. Billy was buttoning his shirt.

It was hot in the evening. The hottest summer in years, everyone said, the hottest ever. At Gerhart's they stood around in big, dusty shoes.

"Shit, it's hot," they told each other.

"Can't get much hotter."

"What'll it be, then?" Gerhart would ask. His idiot son was rinsing glasses.

"Beer."

"Hot enough for you?" Gerhart said as he served it.

They stood at the bar, their arms covered with dust. Across the street was the movie house. Up toward the pass, the sand and gravel pit. There was ranching all around, a macadam plant, men like Wayne Garrich who hardly spoke at all, the bitterness had penetrated to the bone. They were deliberate, their habits were polished smooth. They looked out through the big storelike windows.

"There's Billy."

"Yeah, that's him."

"Well, what do you think?" They laid out phrases in low voices, like bets. Their arms were big as firewood on the bar. "Is he going to it or coming from it?"

The foundation was finished at the beginning of September. There was a little sand where the pile had been, a few specks of gravel. The nights were already cold, the first emptiness of winter, not a light on in town. The trees seemed silent, subdued. They would begin to turn suddenly, the big ones going last.

Harry died about three in the morning. He had been leaning on the cart in the supermarket, behind the stacks, struggling for breath. He tried to drink some tea. He sat in his chair. He was between sleep and waking, the kitchen light was on. Suddenly he felt a terrible, a bursting pain. His mouth fell open, his lips were dry.

He left very little, a few clothes, the Chevrolet filled with tools. Everything seemed lifeless and drab. The handle of his hammer was smooth. He had worked all over, built ships in Galveston during the war. There were photographs when he was twenty, the same hooked nose, the hard, country face. He looked like a pharaoh there in the funeral home. They had folded his hands. His cheeks were sunken, his eyelids like paper.

Billy Amstel went to Mexico in a car he and Alma bought for a hundred dollars. They agreed to share expenses. The sun polished the windshield in which they sat going southward. They told each other stories of their life.